Me, Myself & Irene

20TH CENTURY FOX PRESENTS A CONUNDRUM ENTERTAINMENT PRODUCTION A FARRELLY BROTHERS MOVIE JIM CARREY RENÉE ZELLWEGER "ME, MYSELF & IRENE" CHRIS COOPER ROBERT FORSTER RICHARD JENKINS SONG BY PETE YORN & LEE SHIT MUSIC TIM WILEY & MANISH KAVAL EDITED BY MARC S. FISHER PRODUCTION DESIGNER SIDNEY J. BARTHOLOMEW JR. PHOTOGRAPHY MARK IRWIN, C.S.C., A.S.C. EXECUTIVE PRODUCERS CHARLES B. WESSLER TOM SCHULMAN PRODUCED BY BRADLEY THOMAS & BOBBY FARRELLY & MIKE CERRONE & BOBBY FARRELLY WRITTEN BY PETER FARRELLY & DIRECTED BY BOBBY FARRELLY & PETER FARRELLY

Me, Myself & Irene

A NOVEL BY DAVID JACOBS

BASED ON THE SCREENPLAY BY PETER FARRELLY & MIKE CERRONE & BOBBY FARRELLY

St. Martin's Paperbacks

ME, MYSELF & IRENE

Copyright © 2000 Twentieth Century Fox Film Corporation. All Rights Reserved.
Cover art © 2000 Twentieth Century Fox Film Corporation. All Rights Reserved.

ISBN: 0-312-97636-4

Printed in the United States of America

St. Martin's Paperbacks edition / June 2000

10 9 8 7 6 5 4 3 2 1

Chapter One

CONSIDER THE WORM.

It crawls like a snake, but it's not fast, fanged, or venomous, so it doesn't get any respect. It doesn't even crawl, crawling's too fast. It creeps. When it meets an obstacle, it goes around it. It's spineless, with its nerve endings in its skin. Split one in half, and the two newly created creatures live on, each going on its own way.

If it's that way for a worm, then what about a man?

Consider, then, the strange case of Charlie Baileygates.

On a weekday in late April, in Jamestown, Rhode Island, on a day that had already witnessed many wonders, Charlie Baileygates came home from work early, arriving at his small ranch house in a tidy residential neighborhood of similarly modest homes with neatly tended front lawns.

In fact, Charlie's lawn was substandard for its surroundings. It was covered with dog turds. Which was odd, since Charlie didn't have a dog. His next door neighbor, Ed, had two dogs.

Ed, ruddy-faced, porky, was washing his car in the driveway as Charlie drove up on his motorcycle, slowing, turning into his own driveway.

Neighbor Ed thought little of Charlie's arrival, if it registered at all. Charlie wasn't the kind of guy people paid attention to, generally, except to tsk-tsk or smirk or whatever, whenever he got handed a particularly raw deal—which was often.

Charlie climbed off his motorcycle and crossed to Ed's property, marching forward with a fixed, intent stare. A fifty-yard-stare, looking off into distances that weren't there. Charlie was fortyish, trim, dark-haired, with a rubbery-featured face and long gangling arms and legs.

Staring straight ahead, he passed within a few feet of Ed, who stood in his driveway holding a green garden hose which jetted water. Ed had stopped washing the car at Charlie's approach.

Without the least gesture of greeting or even acknowledgment, without so much as a flickering glance of recognition, Charlie marched past Ed, continuing past him toward the house.

Ed stood there, bemused, puzzled, holding the business end of the hose so that the steady spill of water arched out of the nozzle, spattering on the driveway.

Charlie went into Ed's house, entering through a side door, which Ed had left unlocked when he'd come outside to wash the car. Ed stood there, not so bemused, frankly puzzled, staring at the door through which Charlie had gone, disappearing inside the house.

Ed scratched his head.

A moment later, when Charlie returned, Ed was still standing there, frozen into that same position, holding the hose while water pooled on the asphalt driveway, wetting his shoes.

Charlie was seemingly unchanged, except that he now held a newspaper folded under one arm. Still he ignored Ed, as if Ed wasn't there.

Charlie crossed to the center of Ed's front lawn, dropped his pants and shorts, and squatted down to do his business.

Shortly thereafter, the nearest branch of the Rhode Island State Police received a telephone call, making the complaint that one Charlie Baileygates was currently defecating on neighbor Ed's front lawn—in broad daylight, too!—which was contrary to the laws of the state of Rhode Island.

This was far from the first complaint that had been made today about Charlie. The local branch of the state police was well aware of him. Painfully so.

He was one of their own.

Charlie Baileygates was a state trooper.

Indeed, he was in uniform as he made an unsolicited human fertilizer donation on Ed's front lawn.

Compounding the offense, he was in uniform out of doors minus his headgear, a violation of the department's uniform personal appearance and deportment guidelines.

How had Charlie Baileygates, father of three, dedicated and tireless public servant and longtime professional law enforcement agent, come to the point of taking a crap on his neighbor's front lawn?

Just lucky, you might say. But you'd be wrong. The advent of Charlie's wonderful, terrible new life did not spring into being all at once, like toadstools popping up after a night of early spring rain.

Oh, no.

Charlie's breakdown—or breakthrough, depending on one's point of view—had been years in the making. Eighteen years, at least. Eighteen years of his ego being subjected to crippling psychological maxistress.

Given pressure enough and time, a lump of coal will transform to a diamond, glittering and hard.

Given pressure enough and time, the mind of a man like Charlie will transform to . . . *what?*

One thing was certain—those weren't diamonds that Charlie was depositing in Ed's front yard.

The source of Charlie's trauma lay far in the past, though the wounds were ever fresh. It had begun almost twenty years ago, when Charlie was the most outstanding young trooper in state police ranks, a model of firm-but-fair professional law enforcement, and deeply, truly in love with lovely young Layla Hansen.

And why not? Layla was not only beautiful, she was built. Smart, too. She was the president of the local chapter of Mensa, the braniacs' association.

Charlie may have had his virtues, but he was no braniac. Not for the first time, this realization was brought home one summer day, while she and Charlie were picnicking in a secluded grove in the park, stretched out on a blanket spread on the grass, drinking wine and laughing.

It was a good thing Charlie was a state trooper, because it was illegal to drink wine in the park, or any other alcoholic beverage. But Charlie was off-duty and in civilian clothes, so it was okay.

There they were, Charlie and Layla, two crazy kids in love, and it was better than okay, it was all right.

Layla said, "You have no idea how much I love you, Charlie."

Charlie lay stretched out on his back, head in her lap, looking up at the clouds floating across blue sky. He was chewing on the end of a long toothpick-thin fresh green weed stalk.

He said, "Yeah? Well, if we had to move to Antarctica and we could never come back and you had to eat whale blubber with me for the rest of our lives, would you stay with me?"

She said, "Yeah."

"Sure, that was an easy one. But what if I was

completely paralyzed in a terrible accident and you had to clean up after me and wipe my butt and put drops in my eyes 'cause I couldn't even blink. Would you stay with me then?"

Layla sighed. "I already do that now, Charlie."

He looked embarrassed. "That was only that one time. And I'd prefer for you not to mention it."

"Yes, Charlie."

"Now, what if I was kidnapped and the only way you could get me back was to eat a big huge ball of your worst enemy's boogers and wash it down with a big bucket of John Madden's urine."

"Yes, Charlie, I would, but I'm hoping that doesn't happen."

"Yeah, me too, but it's good to know just in case."

She leaned in and they started to kiss. The weed he was chewing on got in the way. He got it unstuck from between his teeth, but it left his smile green-stained . . .

And so they were wed, in a quaint, old, gray-stone church. The groom was handsome and the bride was beautiful but unblushing as they came out from under the pointed stone archway of the church's main entrance, whisking along the concrete path between applauding, rice-throwing friends and relatives.

Intercepting the happy couple was Charlie's boss, Captain Partington, a craggy-faced, wide-bodied man who kissed the bride and gave Charlie a great big bear hug. As his ribs groaned under the crushing grip, Charlie wondered if he might not have been better off being kissed, too.

Partington was kind of red-faced and breathless himself. He said, "Congratulations, Charlie."

"Thanks, Captain."

The captain watched Charlie and Layla traipse off into the waiting limousine, smiling benevolently at them, still savoring the unexpected taste of Layla's tongue, which she had stuck in his mouth when he'd kissed the bride. Now, *he* was blushing.

The limo driver, one Shonte Jackson, was a taciturn black man, in a dark short-brimmed cap, white shirt, and dark jacket which was stretched at the seams by big, broad shoulders. He stayed in his seat, not moving to assist Charlie and Layla in loading their bags.

The limo rolled away.

Its destination was the newlyweds' love shack, the modest suburban home that Charlie would still be living in, eighteen years later, when he did a nasty on Ed's lawn.

The long limo pulled into the driveway. Charlie and Layla got out and went to the front door, where the bride was carried across the threshold, in traditional fashion.

This was their dream house, their first house together. It wasn't much, but it was heaven. Charlie'd had to go deep into hock to make the down payment, but what the heck?

Layla went deeper into the house, into the bedroom.

Meanwhile, the limo driver appeared at the front door, carrying the newlyweds' bags. Charlie was surprised to note that the driver stood somewhere around three and a half feet tall. He was one of the little people. He'd been sitting up front in the driver's seat the whole time during the trip from the church, so Charlie had been unaware that the other was anything less than standard-issue size.

It threw him, but only for a moment. The driver stood on the front stoop, framed by the open doorway, filling it about halfway as he set down the bags.

Charlie reached into his pockets, only to realize with a start that he was without his wallet. He'd left it in another pair of pants. Leaving him with no money with which to tip the driver.

It was embarrassing. Here it was, his wedding day. He didn't want to look like he was stiffing the driver. That would make him look bad, it'd be bad for all troopers everywhere.

Charlie said, "Uh, excuse me, do you people take checks?"

The driver, Shonte, took it the wrong way. A lifetime of staring into people's crotches had perhaps not left him in the best of tempers.

He bristled, indignant. "Say that again? Do *we people* take checks? You mean, the black man?"

Charlie was instantly embarrassed to have the

other misconstrue his meaning. "No, no, no. I meant your *company*."

The driver was having none of it. "Don't give me that backtracking bullshit. That was a racist slur!"

This was embarrassing. Charlie began, "No, really, I—"

Shonte snapped, "Tell you what, I'll make it easy for you—why don't you just pay me in cotton, or a cartload of watermelons, or how's about a couple of them buckets of fried chickens."

Charlie held up his hands, palms up, in front of him, making warding gestures. "*Hey hey hey*, you're way out of line now."

Drawn by the commotion, Layla appeared. "What's going on?"

Shonte said, "This cat don't believe a nigger knows how to cash a check."

Layla, shocked, blanched. "Charlie! Don't you ever use the N-word in this house!"

"What? I never said anything remotely racist."

A bitter, knowing, ultracynical sneer twisted Shonte's mouth. "So it's the little people thing then?"

Charlie said, *"No."*

"You think just 'cause I'm small you can push me around? Well come on, my friend, let's boogie."

Shonte dropped into a crouch, head ducked, chin pressing his chest, arms reaching and legs spread, ominously circling Charlie like a wrestler looking for an opening to unleash a devastating array of moves. "I'll give you a little lesson in low center of gravity!"

Charlie said weakly, "No, cut it out . . . stop that."

Shonte kept circling, whirling and feinting, making Charlie dizzy just to watch him. "Any time you're feeling a little froggy, go ahead and leap!"

Charlie looked sick. "I don't want to be froggy with you. Look, sir, I'm sorry if you misconstrued—"

"Don't patronize me with that 'sir' crap."

Some kind of threshold had been reached. Shonte went for a weapon, reaching inside his dark unzipped jacket to withdraw a pair of nunchucks, a martial arts device made of two sticks of wood joined by a chain.

His less than dextrous handling of the 'chucks did not make them any less dangerous.

Layla stepped between them. "Stop it, you two!"

She turned to her new husband. "Now, Charlie, let me handle this."

Peering down at the driver's name tag, Layla said, "Excuse me, Mister, um, Jackson, what's your first name?"

"Shonte."

"Shonte, I really do apologize, from my heart. Here, let me walk you to your car."

She and Shonte crossed to the limo, while a crestfallen Charlie picked up the bags and took them inside the house.

Shonte said, "I don't have patience for people who judge books by their cover."

"And you shouldn't have to," Layla said seriously.

Shonte was still nursing a grudge. "Treating me like a dumb shit—who does he think he's talking to? I'm a tenured professor of molecular genetics over at Brown and head of the Boston chapter of Mensa. I'm just driving this limo as a sociological experiment."

Layla eyes lit up. "Mensa? You're kidding. *I'm* president of the Providence chapter.

Shonte looked interested . . .

"Be fruitful and multiply," saith the Lord, and Layla hearkened unto the call, conceiving and growing full with child. When she was full to overflowing, she got hence to the delivery room of the local hospital and prepared to unburden herself.

Charlie was present to witness and share the miracle of life, standing nearby Layla in the delivery room. Weeks of parent-to-be classes hadn't quite prepared Charlie for the reality of the birthing process. It was awful—palpitations, heavy breathing, convulsive spasms, faintness, and even screaming. And that was just Charlie. One of the doctors gave him a sedative and he quieted down some, but he was still in pretty bad shape, his complexion a darker shade of green than the sanitary hospital scrubs that he was wearing.

Nature took its course. The nurses were working

furiously, the doctor was in control, and Layla was writhing in the final throes of creation.

Charlie flinched, but if Layla could take it, so could he, so he stopped covering his eyes with his hands and looked.

Layla gave a final heave, and the do was done, the baby dropping all fat, slick, sassy, and dripping into the doctor's cradling rubber-gloved hands.

Charlie's eyes went wide. So did the doctor's and nurses', but they had professionalism to keep them going and cover up their startlement at what Layla's efforts had wrought.

The baby was a fine healthy specimen, with all ten fingers and all ten toes, bawling lustily when the doctor gave it a slap to welcome it into the world.

The baby was black, unquestionably bearing a proud African-American genetic legacy.

The doctor, a bit nonplussed, said, "It's a . . . um . . . a . . . um . . . oh, boy." He handed the baby to Charlie, the father in name if not of biological generation.

Charlie, in shock, said, "Wow . . . he's so . . . wow."

Layla smiled, a bit sheepishly, then grimaced with a flash of pain. The doctor and nurses grouped around her.

Glancing over his shoulder at Charlie, the doctor said, "Uh . . . you're in luck."

"Hm?"

"There's more than one."

In fact, Charlie was now the proud father-by-proxy of three bouncing baby boys, since Layla had triplets. Charlie rationalized that the babies' hyper-abundance of melanin had been caused by some fluke of nature, some recessive gene back there on the family DNA helix.

Although those nagging doubts were compounded when Layla insisted on naming one of the infants "Shonte Jr." The other two were named Jamal and Lee Harvey.

Charlie was a good soul, and loved those youngsters with a deep and abiding, full-hearted love.

Still, tongues will wag, and under the circumstances, town gossips had a field day speculating about the children's obscure antecedents. Even some of his cop "buddies" were not above needling Charlie on the touchy subject, as was brought home to him during a backyard barbecue he and Layla hosted one fine summer day, attended by other troopers and their families.

Dressed in casual civvies, sport-shirts and slacks, about a half dozen troopers stood off to one corner of the yard, playing lawn darts, or Jarts, as they were called locally. The Jarts were torpedo-shaped brightly colored plastic jobs, about the size of soda bottles, with four fins at one end, and a four inch long steel-tipped point at the other. Little plastic ring markers were set at regular intervals in the square of lawn, denoting scoring areas radiating out from

the bull's-eye. The game was played similarly to
darts, with the players taking turns launching the
Jarts on the marked lawn section, racking up points.

Once everybody'd had a few beers, it wouldn't be
long before the players started amusing themselves
by throwing the Jarts at each other.

At the other end of the backyard, on a concrete
patio near the house, were the trooper wives,
grouped around a couple of pieces of lawn furniture
and a wooden picnic table covered with a red-and-
white checked plastic tablecloth.

A handful of kids ran around the backyard, in and
out of the house.

Now two years old, Jamal, Lee Harvey, and
Shonte Jr. stood naked in a small plastic wading
pool, splashing around under the watchful eyes of
one of the trooper wives, who was looking after the
kids while Layla went inside, returning with a tray
filled with a fresh round of drinks.

Charlie stood over the barbecue grill, wearing an
apron emblazoned with the legend, KISS ME, I'M THE
CHEF. Spatula in hand, he tended the burgers and hot
dogs sizzling on the grill.

Trooper Finneran, a beetle-browed lug with a
refrigerator-shaped body, held an open beer in each
hand as he drifted over to Charlie. "Hey, buddy."

Charlie said, "I hope you brought your appetite."

"Oh, I did," Finneran said, belching. After a
pause, he began, "Charlie, not for nothing, but have

you noticed that those kids of yours have sort of a year-round tan."

Charlie's hand became just a trifle unsteady, wielding the spatula that was working the burgers and franks. He said, "Yeah, well . . . My great-grandmother was Italian, from the south."

Finneran wouldn't let it go. "How about their hair? You see the way the water just beads off it?"

"Yeah, so?" Charlie said, a little bit touchy. "Everybody's hair's a little different. What are you getting at?"

Finneran snorted. "Dammit, Charlie, those kids' dicks are bigger than them hot dogs you're grilling."

Charlie, offended, said, "Hey, knock it off, Finneran. Those are my children you're talking about—"

Captain Partington said, "Finneran!"

Knowing his master's voice, Finneran turned toward the trooper boss. Partington said gruffly, "Get over here, it's your game."

Finneran left Charlie, joining the other troopers. A couple of beers later, the troopers started throwing the Jarts at the ground near each other's feet. That's how it started. Then they started throwing them at each other's feet.

By the time it was done, more than a few of them were limping badly, profoundly grateful that their official duties would not require them to go on walking patrol.

Although he kept a game face on things, Charlie

could not help but occasionally be troubled in the depths of his soul, not by his situation, but by strange tensions and pressures he felt welling up inside his psyche, frightening forerunners of a new kind of outlook that he did not entirely understand.

To ease his worried mind, he sought comfort and guidance from his clergyman, in the inviolate sanctity of the confessional.

Charlie huddled in the intimate dimness of the booth, its low light and grilled commmunicating screen veiling him from the gaze of the priest who sat on the other side of the panel.

The priest said, soft-voiced, interested, "How can I help you, friend?"

Charlie began hesitantly, "There's something powerful bubbling up inside me, Father. I can feel it in there more and more, and I'm afraid if I don't do something . . . some day I'm going to explode."

"Where does his rage come from, my son?"

"I don't know," Charlie said, sighing. "It's a bunch of stuff really. Take my wife, for instance. I love her like no other, but part of me suspects that she may be having an affair. And I'm probably just being paranoid, but I get the feeling that the entire town is laughing at me behind my back."

There was a long pause on the other side of the booth.

Then the priest said, "Charlie . . . that you?"

*   *   *

Soon after, the bottom fell out of Charlie Bailey-gates's world, as Layla took leave of him. She did not leave in secret, in the dead of night, but left by day, under the afternoon sun, placing her suitcases in the trunk of a long, gleaming stretch limo parked in Charlie's driveway.

In the driver's seat, impatiently drumming his fingers on the steering wheel, sat Shonte, propped up on a couple of phone books.

Charlie stood by, devastated, head bowed, shoulders slumped, the corners of his eyes and mouth turned down.

Layla said, not sounding sorry at all, "I'm so sorry, Charlie. Really. But I have to do this. I've found my soul mate."

Charlie vented a squawk of deep emotional pain. "Soul mate? I thought I was your—"

Shonte stuck his head out of the car window and said, "Come on, sweetmeat, let's get a roll on!" He was speaking to Layla.

Layla said, "I don't know what to say, Charlie. I guess the heart just wants what the heart wants."

"But I don't want you to go!"

"This is my heart we're talking about, Charlie, not yours. That is so typical of you, always thinking about yourself first and not about my wants and needs."

Charlie's lower lip quivered. "B-but what happened to loving me from here to Uranus?"

Shonte called out to him, "Don't you be worrying about that. That's mine now."

Layla got into the limo and they drove away. Charlie stood there, watching them go. After they were gone, he shouted, "Well, all I can say is, it's a good thing I didn't have to depend on you to save me if I got kidnapped!"

Layla's leaving left Charlie traumatized with a big ball of hurt. Other men might have broken down and cried, thrown open the window and taken potshots at passersby, or eaten the gun in classic suicidal-cop fashion.

Charlie did none of these things. He just swallowed hard, feeling that slab of gristly, indigestible heartache slide over the lump in his throat, thudding into his belly like an icy paving stone. He locked it all away, and swore that he'd never fall in love again.

But Charlie had forgotten one thing, if he'd ever known it at all—the natural law that states that for every action, there is an opposite and equal reaction.

A law that holds true not only for physics, but for the uncharted depths of the psyche, too.

But such interiorizings were foreign to Charlie, who tried to put it all out of his mind. As if he could!

Life goes on, and he had duties, responsibilities to his family. Layla was gone, but not forgotten, especially as she had neglected to take the kids with her, leaving Charlie alone to raise Jamal, Lee Harvey, and Shonte Jr. by himself.

The random throw of the genetic dice had resulted in Shonte's trait of dwarfism in skipping a generation, so the three youngsters grew to normal height and development for their ages. Happily, the brainy qualities that had rocketed both Shonte and Layla to the heights of the high-IQ Mensa hierarchy had been passed along to their sons.

Charlie took pride in his gifted children, although the extent of their intellectual mastery soon became alarming. One day, when the lads were about nine years old, Charlie had suited up in his trooper uniform and was heading out of his house, on the way to work, when he found the trio hunkered down in the driveway, tinkering with a pile of loose mechanical parts and scraps from variously disassembled machines found around the garage, such as lawnmower motors, bicycle frameworks, and the like.

Charlie said, "Whatcha building, fellas?"

Lee Harvey said, "An airplane, Daddy."

If that wasn't the cutest thing! What could be more charmingly traditional and boyish, than for the lads to be getting together to build a toy airplane.

Beaming, Charlie said, "There's some pretty good-size rubber bands out in my tool box."

The kids stared at him, confused.

It was Charlie's turn for confusion, fueled by panic, when he later came home from work, just in time to see the kids preparing to launch the full-size, ultralight mini-airplane which they'd built in his absence.

The machine's lawn mower motor blatted away, sputtering merrily, spinnning an old window-fan blade that had been pressed into service as a propellor, whirring at the nose of a bicycle-frame body.

It was piloted by Shonte Jr., who sat perched on the bicycle seat, a football helmet placed on his head to serve as a crash helmet. Lee Harvey and Jamal stood on either side of the craft, holding on behind the back of the seat, running forward to add their speed and impetus to help loft the machine on take-off.

Coolly, calmly, taking care not to panic the boys, Charlie communicated his quiet doubts about the wisdom of the enterprise by running forward, waving his arms over his head and screaming, "NO, NO, NO, DON'T YOU TRY TO TAKE OFF IN THAT THING!"

Liftoff was narrowly averted, and the maiden flight aborted, to the disgust of the lads, who insisted that the home-crafted miniplane would indeed have taken wing and soared.

Charlie thought so, too, which made him doubly glad he'd stopped it, though what that whirling propellor had done to his spiffy trooper's uniform was not a pretty thing. He counted himself lucky to have emerged with all his digits intact.

Charlie prided himself on being a progressive influence, so aside from their formal schooling, he took pains to make sure the boys didn't lose touch with their own cultural heritage.

He and the lads were in the family room, seated around the television, enjoying some of the high-quality diversified programming dispensed by the tube.

Plastic wrapping crinkled as Shonte Jr. fed himself from a pack of fried pork chop rinds, yet one more entry in a round of snack-food snacking that he'd recently begun in earnest.

Charlie said, "Shonte Jr., how can you keep eating that crap without ever gaining a pound?"

Shonte Jr. shrugged. "I don't know. Just lucky, I guess."

"Incredible."

On-screen, on a variety show, a tuxedoed baritone was warbling his way through an operatic aria.

Charlie leaned forward in his seat, impressed. "Can you believe that singing? That's Gomer Pyle."

And so it was, for the star of the hit TV series about the goofy marine had hidden talents, not least of which was a golden throat.

The kids, bored, stirred restlessly. Lee Harvey said, "Daddy, can we watch Richard Pryor on HBO?"

"Richard Pryor?" Charlie had to think a moment, before the name clicked. "Oh, he's that fella I saw on Merv. Sure, he seems like a real card."

But the cable TV routine was quite a different kettle of fish from the whitebread, sanitized routine he'd been laying down on the Mervelous Griffin broadcast. The standup comedian had barely launched into one of the pieces from his comedy concert, a raunchy monologue about a white john, a black pimp, and three whores on a double bed, before a nervous Charlie was looking for the remote control, to click the channel to more innocuous fare.

But the kids were laughing, and when he saw how much fun they were having, Charlie relented and even began to laugh along himself.

Years passed, and the kids came into their own, growing into three near-adult teenagers who between them weighed nearly 800 pounds of big, black, young manhood. More than a third of that poundage was totalled by Shonte Jr., who'd really blimped up over the course of time, as those fried pork chop rinds caught up to him.

One thing remained unchanged, however: The deep and abiding affection that led dad and lads to cluster around the old cathode-ray tube, enjoying some of the finest and most high-quality diversified TV product.

Or as Charlie put it, as the family absorbed HBO's latest comedy concert, "That Chris Rock is a funny motherfucker."

Less funny, indeed no laughing matter, were the changes working their way deep down inside Charlie, below-stairs there, down in the psychic basement. Lee Harvey, Shonte Jr., and Jamal were all healthy and normally well-adjusted, at least as far as teenagers go. The same could not be said of Charlie.

Behavioral scientists had explicated the problem long ago, experimenting with lab rats. They'd take a rat and teach it to press a lever that would give them food. Then, when the rat was thoroughly associated with the process, the lab boys would throw it a curve by rigging up the lever so that every time the rat threw it, it gave the rodent a painful electric shock. And no food. The rat had to press the lever to eat, but when it did, it got a shock. Eventually, after having tried and failed a number of times, the rat would go off by itself and have a mental breakdown.

For long years, since those initial Layla-caused traumas, Charlie had been soaking up stress. As a nice, decent guy who genuinely liked people, he could count on being the repository of more emotional garbage than a toxic-waste dump.

He soaked it up, all of it, every bit, spewing none of it out. Down deep in the well of his mind it was bubbling around like hot oatmeal, churning, heaving massively with its own restless pseudolife.

A radioactive pile of seething resentment.

The day it achieved critical mass, Charlie made his breakthrough.

First, though, came the barracks locker room incident. That shoved a few graphite rods into the old plutonium pile.

The state police branch substation in the Jamestown area was a shoebox-shaped building parked alongside the interstate highway. Charlie had just finished a day shift and was coming off duty. He went into the locker room to change.

It seemed empty. The other guys going off-shift must have not yet arrived at the station.

At the head of an aisle between the lockers, Charlie discovered Trooper Finneran standing bending forward over an open locker, taking some bills out of a wallet, which he then returned to the pocket of a pair of pants, placing them in the locker.

It was not Finneran's locker.

Charlie had caught Finneran red-handed, in the act of stealing from a brother officer. Finneran couldn't have looked more guilty, standing hunched over with a fistful of pilfered cash, as motionless as if he was posing for a picture.

Charlie had a curious feeling of unreality. He said, "Finneran, what the hell are you doing in Captain Partington's locker?"

Finneran was stumped for an answer. His face was bright and shining, his eyes glittered. He ran a blunt-tipped tongue across liver lips. He said, "I, uh . . . I'm his secret Santa."

Not even Charlie could swallow that one. "It's May."

"Yeah, so? I'm planning ahead, snooping around to see if there's anything he might need."

"Looks to me like he might be needing some cash, seeing as how you cleaned him out," Charlie said, putting his hands on his hips, not backing off.

Finneran changed his tune, began wheedling. He blinked rapidly, wetness showing in his eyes. He whined, "Look, man, I'm sorry, but I'm going through a hard time and I'm not myself. I caught my wife cheating on me and it's driving me nuts."

Charlie frowned. "I thought she caught you."

"Whatever. Our marriage isn't perfect, okay? Is that what you want to hear?"

Charlie was at a loss what to do.

Perhaps sensing the other's uncertainty, Finneran argued his case harder. He stood with his big hands held out, palms up.

He said, "I'm going through a tough time, man. You've been there. Now I'm begging you not to turn me in."

Charlie, thinking it over, was starting to weaken. "Look, Finneran, I'm paid to uphold the—"

"It was out of character. I guess I was just calling out for help—and now I got it . . . from you, my best friend."

"*I'm* your best friend?"

"Pathetic, huh?"

Charlie, torn, softened. "All right . . . I won't tell. But put the money back and you better get some—"

All at once, as if a switch had been thrown, Finneran's entire demeanor altered, changing from cowering guilt to whooping triumph. Pale eyes glinted in his flushed red face as he held his fists in the air, shaking them, then clapping as if his team had just scored the extra point.

He said, "Hah! That's it, boys. Pay up!"

Four more state troopers popped their heads out of the shower stalls, where they'd been hiding, watching the whole thing. It was all a setup.

There was Pritchard, Neely, and two other guys. Pritchard, hatchet-faced and beady-eyed, was particularly teed-off. Pissed.

He said, "Thanks a lot, Charlie. You just cost us each twenty bucks."

Ever in command, master of the situation, gape-mouthed Charlie could only say, "Whuh?"

Finneran said, "I bet these pigeons that you were the worst trooper on the force. Talk about a sucker bet! HAW!"

Pritchard said, disgusted, "How could you let him slide after he broke into the captain's locker?"

Trooper Neely pressed his lips in tight-mouthed disdain. "Rhode Island State Troopers hold themselves to a higher standard than that. I'm not sure you've still got what it takes to wear this uniform."

Pritchard shook his head, more in pity than anger. "What the hell's gotten into you, Charlie? You used to be a good cop, but ever since . . . well, you know . . . you've let everyone walk all over you."

Neely said, "You're an embarrassment to the force, Charlie."

That was the last word. The troopers exited the locker room, leaving Charlie alone.

*   *   *

The next day, *the* day, in early morning, Charlie's three sons were up and at their various endeavors. Seated at the kitchen table, his schoolbooks spread out in front of him, laboring over his homework, was Shonte Jr., whose incredibly obese form caused the kitchen chairs to groan dangerously under him. He sat on two chairs, one for each butt cheek. Even so, his perch was far from rock-steady.

Beyond the open doorway, in the den opposite, Jamal sat facing a computer screen, fingers pecking out commands on the keyboard. He had a hard, long face and cold eyes and a tight straight ruler-line mouth.

In a corner, Lee Harvey was working out, pumping serious iron, the veins on his bull-neck and thickly muscled arms sticking out like snakes.

Shonte Jr. balled up a piece of notebook paper he'd been working on, and tossed it in the trash. "Damn. I can't figure out the atomic mass of this motherfuckin' deuteron."

Jamal came into the kitchen, looking over Shonte Jr.'s broad sloping shoulders at the pages of textbook equations. He said, "Shit, that's simple. Tell me this—what's a deuteron made of?"

Shonte Jr. said, "A proton and a neutron."

"Then what's this motherfuckin' electron doing over here?"

Shonte Jr. chewed that over, scratching his head

with the eraser end of a pencil. Finally, he looked up, shrugging.

Irked by his obtuseness, Jamal snapped, "Well, get it the fuck outta there!"

In the other room, Lee Harvey set down the barbells, the house shuddering slightly when they hit the floor, even though he'd been careful to let them down easy. He moseyed into the kitchen to see what the fuss was about.

Shonte Jr., trying to put it together, said, "Okay, so I add up the atomic masses of the proton and neutron, I see's that, but what do I do with the gatdamn electron? Can I bring it over here?"

Jamal raised his eyes to the ceiling in a help-me-Lord kind of gesture. His lip curling with contempt, he said, "Enrico Fermi'd roll in his motherfuckin' grave if he heard dat shit."

Playing peacemaker, Lee Harvey said, "Jamal, give my man some slack."

"I'm just trying to help him save face. He keep axing questions like that, peoples gonna think he stupid!"

There was something to that. Lee Harvey nodded, clamming up.

Charlie entered, dressed for work in his trooper's uniform. Dark circles ringed his eyes. He hadn't slept well the night before, endlessly replaying the locker room incident in his head.

Still, he tried to put the best face on things, smiling for the sake of the kids. " 'Mornin', guys."

"Hey, Daddy," the trio said, all at once.

Looking around at the scene in the kitchen, Charlie said, "What's all the commotion?"

Jamal said, "Just school shit and shit."

Charlie poured himself a cup of coffee. He said fondly, "And how's my little guy doing?"

The 300-plus-pound little guy, Shonte Jr., said, "Struggling, Daddy. This quantum physics is confusing. If I don't buckle down, I'm gonna get myself another B-plus."

Lee Harvey said, "He so dumb he think calculus a gatdamn emperor."

Shonte Jr. said, "Yeah, well, you thinks polypeptides a motherfucking toothpaste!"

Father and sons all enjoyed a hearty laugh over that one. But Charlie wasn't laughing when he exited the house by himself, stepping outside into the late-April early-morning sunlight.

Inwardly steeling himself to once more face his fellow troopers, he was distracted by something disturbing as he headed down the driveway toward his motorcycle.

Two mighty dogs, a Great Dane and an Afghan hound, were both squatting down over Charlie's front lawn, each of them taking a mighty crap. That this was no more chance occurrence, but rather part of a lengthy and ongoing process, was demonstrated by the many other piles of crap littering the front yard. It was like a cow pasture for dogs.

They were Ed's dogs. Their master stood nearby,

gazing at them fondly as they finished up their business, trotting back on to his property.

Charlie's eye was alerted not to their presence, but rather to the absence of something else, his morning newspaper.

He said, " 'Mornin', Ed."

"Charlie."

"Uh, Ed, have you seen my paper today?"

"My kid Duke's got it in the shitter."

"Oh. Well if he could just throw it on my porch when he's done."

Ed, irked, demanded, "You can't get one at work?"

For an instant, the other's face set in hard lines, and there was something cold and brightly glinting in his eyes. But in a few heartbeats, it passed, leaving behind ordinary, everyday Charlie Baileygates, good neighbor Charlie who replied, "Yeah . . . I suppose I could."

Remembering somehow to smile, he climbed on his motorcycle and drove away.

Jamestown was a small, sleepy town with stone churches, white steeples, and lots of red-brick buildings. At either end of Main Street stood a bank, each with a Greek Revival columned front. Between them, various commercial buildings lined the street, which broadened at the center to encompass a small oval round of grass topped by a Civil War monument.

Today, Charlie was on town patrol. Midmorning sunlight slanted down Main Street as he stopped his motorcycle beside a Buick parked nose-in at the curb, opposite the barbershop.

Charlie eyed the car, then looked at his wristwatch, frowning. He wheeled his machine off to one side, out of the way, and climbed down, crossing the sidewalk to the barbershop and going inside.

The place smelled sweet, from the combined scents of all the stuff in the different-colored bottles lining the glass shelves under a long mirror covering the upper half of one of the walls.

Freddie the barber had a moose-shaped head, with neat thinning hair plastered to a bony skull. He wore a mint-green, high-collared barber's tunic and circled eight-year-old Timmy, scissors working as he snipped the towheaded youngster's hair.

Seated off to the side, at opposite ends of a card table, playing backgammon, were Dick McGinn and his buddy, Jack.

Dick McGinn was a nattily dressed realtor with pointed eyebrows, puffy eye pounches, and sagging though well-barbered jowls. Jack was a good looking younger guy, handsome and athletic, dressed in casually expensive sport clothes.

George, a roly-poly, bowling pin-shaped guy, stood beside the shop's front window, looking out at the human traffic going by along the sidewalk.

Charlie entered. Freddie the barber said, "Hey, Charlie."

Timmy said, politely, "Hi."

Charlie said, "Hiya, Freddie. Hiya, guys." Freddie nodded. Neither Dick McGinn or Jack looked up from their game board. George was oblivious, transfixed by an approaching vision.

With genuine enthusiasm, he cried, "Hey, Freddie, look at the rack on this one."

Freddie set his scissors down on the counter, rushing to the window, craning for a look. Dick and Jack put their backgammon on hold, drifting over to the window. After a pause, Charlie joined the others.

The object of their attention was an extraordinarily attractive young woman with huge breasts, who was pushing a baby carriage along the sidewalk.

Dick McGinn pursed his lips in a soundless whistle. "Now we're talking!"

George, sweaty, panting, said, "Looks like a dead heat in a zeppelin race."

Even freckle-faced, towheaded little Timmy had joined the viewing gallery lined up at the front window. He said, "Oh, yeah, that's the way Daddy likes it."

Taking the high road, in a manly kind of scoutmaster way, Charlie said, "Guys, go easy. She's a mom."

They looked at him like he was from Mars—but only after the curvaceous honey-hootered big momma had passed by, wiggling her rounded shapely rump away into the distance down the sidewalk.

All drifted back to their original positions, little Timmy hopping up into the barber's chair, Freddie picking up his scissors and returning to work, Dick and Jack sitting back to their game. George stayed where he was, stuck like a barnacle to the window frame, eyeballing the outside street scene.

Back to business is what Charlie's body language said, as he went over to the backgammon players. Clearing his throat, he said, "Say, Dick, sorry to trouble you like this, but your car's going to have to be moved."

Not looking up, Dick said, "Okay, I'll be done here in another ten or fifteen minutes."

This didn't sit well with Charlie, who stood a little straighter, squaring his shoulders. "Um, I hate to be a stickler, but you know the law says you can't park in one place for more than an hour, and you've been there . . ."

At this point Charlie once more checked his watch, recalibrating the elapsed parking time.

". . . Going on three days now," he calculated.

Dick, thoughtful, sighed. "All right, all right, the law's the law."

He tossed something at Charlie, which Charlie reflexively caught, plucking it out of empty air to discover that he now held Dick's car keys.

Once more absorbed in his game, Dick said offhandedly, "Park it out behind the grocery store, will ya, Charlie?"

Charlie stared at the keys, then back at Dick. "Yeah . . . sure."

Outside, a few doors away from the barbershop stood a grocery store, the local convenience Kwikee Mart. In front of it, out in the street, a nine-year-old girl, angel-faced, with blond pigtails, was jumping rope.

Charlie moved toward her, his protective instincts aroused. He said gently, "Sweetie, that's kind of dangerous. Why don't you take it up on the sidewalk, away from the cars."

The moppet said snippily, "My dad says you're a joke and I don't have to listen to you."

She kept on jumping rope.

Charlie was hesitant, unsure. "Well, your dad's entitled to his opinion—but I am an officer of the law . . . by all rights, I could really . . . If I wasn't busy . . ."

The little girl continued jumping rope, ignoring Charlie as if he wasn't there. After a while, it got to him.

"Just be careful," he said, walking away and shaking his head.

He went into the grocery store, picking up a newspaper and a few other items and meandering over to the checkout counter. One or two people were ahead of him, so it only took fifteen minutes or so for the clueless kid working the register to ring them up, bag their packs, and get them out of there.

Only a quarter hour. Pretty good for this store, and now it was Charlie's turn in line.

Before he could edge into position, up rushed Mrs. Bittman, a bulky and assertive citizen with a pitbull face and a Michelin Tire Man body. What she lacked in beauty, she made up for with an absence of charm and the social graces.

She didn't so much talk as bray. "Excuse me, would you mind if I kind of jumped in front of you? I'm in a real rush."

Charlie looked at her. She held only a loaf of bread and a quart of milk, and since he really wasn't in a hurry, or at least not as much of a hurry as she, why, it would only be the polite and gentlemanly thing to do, yielding place of position to her and letting her go through first.

Expansive, generous to a fault, he invited, "Oh, um, no, you go right on ahead, Mrs. Bittman."

She bawled, "Over here, kids!"

On cue, where they'd been waiting for her signal, were her two children, standing poised with a shopping cart crammed over the top with groceries, a mountain of goods. Swift off their mark, the kids shoved the cart forward, pushing it ahead of Charlie and giving him a painful knock on the shinbone.

He yelped. "Hey!"

Mrs. Bittman and her bratty duo shoved ahead, now oblivious to him.

Charlie had a mindquake. Something in his think-machine gave a grinding lurch, throwing the entire mechanism out of whack. Slipping gears.

Charlie was feverish. He couldn't catch his breath. There was a roaring in his ears. People's faces looked distorted, as though seen through a fish-eye lens. Not that most of them had been any prize to start with.

Where had that come from? That wasn't him. He, Charlie, liked people. He tried to see the good in everybody.

He didn't feel too good. He felt like he was going to pass out. He put a hand on the counter to support himself as his vision blurred and his knees got shaky. His eyes were muddy and his complexion was graying.

His head sagged, too heavy for the neck that held it. His eyes were heavy-lidded, almost closed. His head swayed from side to side, like a too-heavy blossom on a too-slender stalk. His face looked the color and consistency of putty.

Just when it seemed he would pass out, he suddenly came to, snapping into full attention, rigid, quivering with barely suppressed energies.

Talk about a Jekyll/Hyde transformation!

Charlie was gone. Whoever, whatever now looked out from behind Charlie's eyes was not Charlie. The whole cast of his face had changed. It was mobile, weasely, shifty-eyed, with elastic features and a loose, expressive rubber-lipped mouth.

He looked sneaky, sly. Though possibly not quite as sly as he thought himself.

It was the face of a wiseguy, a troublemaker.

The Un-Charlie.

The trooper turned a cold eye on Mrs. Bittman's heaped mound of groceries in the shopping cart, his keenly appraising gaze instantly fastening on an item that she had sought, in vain, to bury deep.

Rolling up his cuff, he plunged his hand into the groceries, plucking out with unerring accuracy a bottle of Vagasav Vaginal Salve personal feminine hygiene enhancer, deodorizing agent, and God knows what else.

Leering, holding the bottle high, the label prominently displayed with a skill that would have done a professional pitchman proud, the sneaky guy said, "Vagasav, huh?"

He then gave Mrs. Bittman an incredibly lewd wink, screwing up the side of his face like Popeye. "Little extra cheese on the taco?"

It took her a moment to catch her breath long enough to respond. "Excuse me?"

He said, "You're excused."

She blurted, "Charlie, what's wrong? You're talking so strange!"

"Not Charlie," he said. "Hank."

"Huh?"

"No, Hank. As in, Hank's for the memories." Charlie/Hank raised the Vagasav bottle higher, studying it intently from various angles.

He said, "There's no tag on this. Let me help you out."

Reaching over, he snagged the checkout counter microphone, holding it to his mouth. "Price check on Vagasav. Price check on Vagasav. Aisle five."

His eerily amplified voice boomed and echoed in the store, laden with distorted metallic overtones. Shoppers looked up, wondering.

He spoke into the mic, shaking the walls with the big broadcast. "Red alert! We've got a customer down here with a full-on Fallopian fungus. She's baking a loaf of bread down here and I think it's sourdough.

"That is all. This station is now signing off."

Hank, the stranger inside Charlie's skin, set down the microphone on the counter, smiling toothily at Mrs. Bittman, whose lead-colored face was frantically searching, looking around for someplace, anyplace, into which she could crawl until the whole horrible humiliating situation went away.

Hank went away, exiting the building, conveniently forgetting to pay for the newspaper and other few items he'd walked out with. In the excitement of the moment, no store personnel thought to call him on it, nor would any of them have bothered to confront him if they had thought of it. Nobody was sticking his neck out for the lousy minimum wage that the store was paying.

Besides, there was something off-putting about Hank/Charlie, something that said, *Live wire—do not touch.*

Unfortunately for local businessman and Opti-

.mists' Club President Earl Shugsider, the advent of Hank was a thing unknown to him, as he walked past the front of the grocery store, approaching the dependable and unassuming trooper he knew as Charlie.

Earl said, beaming, "Hey, big guy, ya hear my son Billy got the lead in the school musical?"

Hank said, "Well, then I guess he likes the cock after all, huh?"

Earl did a double take, unsure that he'd heard what he thought he'd heard. While he was thinking it over, Hank went away.

The trouble with Jamestown was that too many people had been getting away with too much for too long, without even getting called on it. Hank was on a mission to clean up the town and he didn't care if his hands got a little dirty doing it.

First for that little jump-roping scamp. Hank caught her standing on a step at the base of the town's water fountain, bending over the fountain so she could take a drink. Coming up behind her, Hank held her face down in the water spewing from the nozzle, washing her face in it.

It wasn't pretty, but the name of the game was proactive law enforcement. Not to mention payback.

He said, "Still want to jump rope in the street, huh?"

When he let her come up for air, gasping, sputtering, she choked, "Why are you doing this, Charlie?"

"The name's Hank, fuckface, and I suggest you use it."

She'd been told and told good. He let her go, stalking off.

It was a lovely day in the park. The bosomy young mom who'd strutted and jiggled her stuff in front of the barber shop was now seated in the shade, on a park bench. She was reading a magazine, with the baby carriage standing angled beside her.

Imagine her surprise when Hank strolled up to the park bench, suddenly contorting himself to put his head in her lap, face-up, a head which he immediately stuffed under and up inside her blouse.

Surprise turned to outrage soon after as, recovering from paralyzing shock, she disengaged her nipple from Hank's suckling mouth.

He looked up at her, lips ringed by a moistly glistening white mustache.

He said, "Got milk?"

Back at the barber shop, things were pretty quiet, little changed from before. Dick McGinn and Jack were still idling over their backgammon, Freddie had finished up barbering little Timmy, and was about to give him a brisk brushing with a whisk broom, and George still stood beside the window, gawking at the passing parade.

Jack made his move on the red-and-tan board. "Your turn, Dick."

Dick looked up for an instant, rubbing his head.

George stiffened, squawking. Dick glanced with casual curiosity, over at the other.

George threw himself backward, away from the window.

A swift shadow of something large and bulky filled the barbershop's window, but only for an instant, resolving itself into Dick's brand-new Buick, no longer illegally parked but now in motion, driving forward across the sidewalk straight at Freddie the barber's front window, and through it.

There was a sound of screeching tires and the engine's roar as the car leaped forward. Dick recoiled, horrified, still clutching the game dice which he'd been about to throw.

The plate glass window disintegrated, imploding in a merry tinkling shower of broken glass, as the Buick drove through it, ramming into the shop.

The car's front bumper halted a few inches short of the backgammon table, in a cloud of powdered plaster, dust, and debris raining down from the ringing rafter beams.

The driver's-side door sliced open and out popped what looked to the others in the barber shop as Trooper Baileygates, but was nothing less than the Anti-Charlie, Hank. Hank circled around the front of the car, still wearing a milk mustache over his mobile smirking mouth, as he tossed Dick his car keys.

Dick was so stunned that he didn't even try to catch them. They hit his chest and bounced off, falling on the floor.

Hank said, "Here you go, Dick. I parked it for you."

Strutting back over to the car, Hank placed one foot on the front bumper, as he reached into his back pocket and whipped out his official ticket book, flipping back the pages and filling in the vital facts on the summons he was now writing up.

When he was done, he slapped the ticket on the cracked, spider-webbed windshield of Dick's Buick.

He told its owner, "You got a headlight out."

By now, the snowballing effect of Hank's malicious spree had set the machinery of justice in motion, as the local state police's station's dispatcher was besieged at her front desk with an ever-increasing volume of complaint calls from irate or alarmed citizens.

The dispatcher, a female trooper named Maryann, finished writing down the information from the latest call and slammed the phone down. She rose, coming around her desk, starting for the captain's office down the hall.

Before she had taken another step, the phone began ringing again. Ignoring it, she hurried forward, scurrying into Captain Partington's office.

Partington looked up from his desk, frowning, his scowl dissolving in the face of Maryann's evident distress.

The lady dispatcher wailed, "Captain, something's wrong with Charlie!"

Partington got in his patrol car, tracking the wayward trooper by the flurry of complaint calls. He found his man, arriving while the Hank Formerly Known as Charlie was taking a dump on neighbor Ed's lawn.

Which brings us full circle.

Hank had officially arrived.

He squatted over the lawn, pants and shorts down around his ankles, intently studying a folded newspaper.

Neighbors stood nearby, but not too closely, clustered in hushed knots. Captain Partington's RISP cruiser was the first police car on the scene. Not the first police vehicle, though, since Charlie's official motorcyle had gotten there earlier.

Partington looked out the window, not liking what he saw. This wasn't the public image that the department liked to present.

He climbed out of his car, putting his hat on. Taking a deep breath, he moved past the gathering crowd toward the front lawn.

He approached Charlie/Hank cautiously. He said, "Uh . . . do you mind telling me what you're doing?"

Hank glanced up, very matter of fact. "Crossword puzzle. What's a four-letter word for evacuate?"

There was nothing the captain had to say about that. After a pause, he said, "Can I have a word with you . . . in my car?"

"Sure thing," Hank said cheerily. "I'll just snap this off."

He rose, pulling up his pants. "So how can I help you, flatfoot?"

Grouped in front of Charlie's house, where they'd been standing watching in frozen astonishment, were his three sons.

Shonte Jr. said, "*Damn.* What's up with that?"

Jamal said, "You think Dad be getting too much stress?"

Lee Harvey said, "I say he be getting too much Shredded Wheat by the motherfuckin' look of it."

They and the rest of the neighbors watched as Partington gently herded Charlie/Hank into the police cruiser and drove away.

Chapter Two

THE DOCTORS SHOT UP HANK WITH MEGASEDA-
tives and when he woke up again, he was Charlie,
groggy and bewildered as to how he'd gotten into
the hospital. Had he been in an accident or something, the trauma causing him to forget what had
happened to him?

He was even more bewildered to discover that he
was in a lockdown ward for potentially violent patients in a mental hospital.

He, Charlie Baileygates, crazy? Why, it was—
crazy! That's what it was, crazy!

He told all the staffers, the doctors and nurses and
orderlies, that he was fine, perfectly normal. They
kept him under observation anyway, for the better
part of a week.

There were no more recurrences of his Hank
persona, and since they needed the space for more
disturbed patients, and mainly because his hospital-

ization benefits were starting to run out, they released him.

He stayed home over the weekend, resting. On Monday morning, he put on his uniform and went to work. But Charlie did not go out on patrol, according to routine. Instead, he attended a closed-door meeting in Captain Partington's office. The subject: Charlie's fitness to return to duty. Also present in his capacity as the station's second-in-command was Finneran.

Partington, Finneran and Charlie were seated around a table. Charlie sat at one end, hands folded on the tabletop in front of him, as he expectanctly eyed the other two at the opposite end of the table.

Partington's chair creaked as he leaned forward, trying to look concerned, avuncular. The gleam of his eye was like that of a benevolent crocodile, one that'd eaten recently and wasn't too hungry again yet.

Finneran looked like what he was, which was a horse's ass.

With manly gruffness and the attitude of a plain-spoken man who speaks his mind, Finneran spoke plainly. "You're a lunatic, Charlie! That's what the best shrinks in New England are saying: You are a nutcase."

Wincing slightly, Captain Partington said, "Finneran, how about a little compassion here, huh? Jesus Christ, this is a fellow human being we're talking to here, a brother officer. Charlie, what we're trying to say here, in a nice way, is that you've got a major screw loose."

Charlie gave it a moment's thought, while the others watched intently, waiting for him to speak. Finally, he unburdened himself, saying, "Hm?"

Partington began again, nodding pleasantly. "The doctors, they've diagnosed you as having a split personality."

Finneran chimed in, "A schizo."

Charlie still had trouble swallowing the diagnosis. "I . . . I don't know what to say, Chief. I wish I could remember what happened, but it's all a blank."

"That's because, according to this report, it wasn't you it was happening to. It was . . . this other guy," the captain said earnestly.

Finneran said, "Hank."

Charlie looked at him, mouth gaping. "Huh?"

Finneran said, "He said his name was Hank." That was something Finneran wasn't likely to forget. Charlie was beneath contempt, but Hank, to tell the truth, was just a little bit . . . not *scary* actually, but, well, unpredictable. Volatile.

Well, scary.

Partington continued, "And apparently Hank is trying to get out."

That was a hell of a thing. Charlie, disbelieving, demanded, "What do you mean, *out?* How'd he get in?"

Finneran said, "You created him." With the emphasis on "you." As if Charlie was to blame.

Was he? He was unsure himself.

Partington explained, "You created him by not dealing with your problems, Charlie. Ever since . . . er, you know . . . you've been avoiding confrontations. But this guy inside . . ."

"Hank," Finneran said, determined to keep the heat on Charlie's chaotic alter-ego.

". . . He doesn't," the captain said. "The doctors feel that this character was created out of necessity. You never stick up for yourself and obviously it's taken a toll."

Charlie tried to look bright-eyed, enthusiastic, and perfectly normal. He was trying too hard. The glint in his eyes would have unnerved the others even if the psychotic Hank-episode had never occurred.

Charlie adopted the air of a reasonable man. "Well, they're entitled to their expert opinions, but I don't agree. I stick up for myself all the time. Right, Finneran? Come on, help me out here."

Finneran scoffed. "Come off it, Charlie. You never say what's on your mind."

Partington asked, "Charlie, why didn't you take a vacation after Layla left."

The mention of Layla's name could still give Charlie a pang, and it showed on his face. Some of his sureness left him and he became evasive, blustering.

He said, "Well, why would I? Wives walk out on their husbands every day in this country. That's no reason to shortchange the department." His voice cracked with emotion. "I mean it's not like I had the flu," he added weakly.

Partington and Finneran exchanged glances. Not ungently, Partington said, "Have you picked up your medication, Charlie?"

Charlie had regained some of his composure. "Yeah, but I don't like it. It gives me cottonmouth something terrible."

"Well, you're gonna have to take it anyway. Dr. Rabinowitz assured us that if you do, everything will be fine."

"Yeah. Well, if that'll make you guys happy . . ."

Outside, muffled by the closed door, came the sounds of a commotion at the front desk. There was scuffling, then a woman shouted, "Hey, let go!"

It wasn't a happy sound, and even ten days after Hank's rampage, they were still uneasy around the state police station house.

Partington, Finneran, and Charlie rose, going to the door, opening it and stepping through it into the hall, where they could see the front desk area.

Trooper Pritchard was bringing in a prisoner, a handcuffed young woman. She was in her late twenties, madder than a wet hen—and very beautiful. Lovely, lithe, and ripely curved. Her hair was in disarray, her face was flushed, and her eyes were sharp, angry, and maybe just a little scared.

No matter what, she was a knockout, a dish, a peachareeno.

And very much the well-spoken young lady. Seeing Captain Partington, she shouted, "Listen, this is a bunch of horseshit!"

She'd shouted close to Pritchard's ear, and he flinched. He had his hands on her shoulders, steering her around the floor. He said, "All right, all right. Take it easy."

She said, "Could you maybe get your goddamn hands off me!"

Partington advanced, throwing the long shadow of his imposing authority across the scene, with Finneran and Charlie trailing after.

The captain said, "Pritchard, what's going on here?"

Pritchard said, "Captain, her name's Waters, Irene P. I pulled her over on 95—broken taillight. Turns out she's got an outstanding warrant in upstate New York."

Irene said, "Bullshit!"

She might even have believed it, for all the vehemence with which she said it. But that was nothing new to the troopers. Everybody was innocent, at least in their own estimation, once the law had put the arm on them. If you believed the suspects, the police had never, ever arrested a guilty person. Sure, they were all innocent, right up until the deals were cut at the plea bargaining session with the state prosecutor.

Partington defused some of the tension of the situation, with Irene quickly calming down to where it was judged safe to remove her from the restraining handcuffs. She chafed her slim wrists, rubbing them where the cuffs had left red marks on her smooth pink skin.

Partington took her over to one side of the administrative area and had her sit down while he had Maryann run a check on any warrants outstanding.

Sure enough, one came up. Partington sat there with the computer printout in his hand, scanning the the text.

Irene, shocked, said, "Warrant?! For what?"

Partington's manner was serious, almost grave. He said, "Hit and run. An injured pedestrian filed the complaint."

Irene's intense irritation now spiked into still-higher registers. "That's ridiculous, I've never been in an accident in my life."

Partington shrugged. "I just got off the phone with the New York State Patrol. They don't seem to think it's so ridiculous."

With a show of difficulty, Irene got her temper under control. She switched tracks, saying brightly, "Tell you what: Let's just fast forward to the part where I'm naked on the school bus so I can wake up from this nightmare."

Partington, silent, eyed her blandly. Irene leaned forward, speaking very carefully, enunciating clearly. She said, "Someone has made a mistake."

That was one thing both she and the trooper boss could agree on. There the common ground ended, and their interests diverged. All Partington knew, or needed to know, was that the New York State Police had a warrant out for the suspect in connection with a hit-and-run, and that he had that suspect in custody.

The captain was nobody's fool, but damn it all, the woman's manner was so convincing. The warrant was out of a place called Messina. Messina, New York.

"Miss Waters, were you in Messina, New York, last Friday, May the second?"

"Well, sure . . ." Her voice trailed off. Her gaze went slightly off-focus as she sat there, remembering.

Finally she said, "I've been living there for the past two years, but I was never in any accident. I'm on my way to visit my sister on Martha's Vineyard. Can't I just handle this by mail?"

"Unfortunately, Miss Waters, I'm not the one you have to convince. If there's been a mistake, you'll have to clear it up in Messina."

Irene, exasperated, said, "Wait a second, are you telling me I have to drive all the way back to western New York?"

"No, ma'am."

"Well, thank God for that!"

"We'll have one of our troopers escort you," the captain said equably. Movement in the corridor attracted his attention.

Charlie stood there at the water cooler, taking a pill. It was a large one, a big fat horse pill. He put it on his tongue, gulping it down with some water, his Adam's apple bobbing.

Maybe it was psychological, but as soon as he'd swallowed the pill, his mouth had gone dry. Bone dry. It felt like it was coated with powered salt-crackers. His tongue was thick, heavy.

He started working it, rolling his tongue and working his lips, making smacking sounds.

Irene slumped even lower in her chair, dispirited.

Studying Charlie, Captain Partington thoughtfully stroked his blocky chin.

"Yes, Miss Waters, you'll have a trooper escort."

Irene groaned.

While Irene sat stewing in the Rhode Island State Police's Jamestown area station, a couple of hundred miles away, in upstate New York, not far from the Canadian border, in Messina, at the Mississaugua Country Club, a foursome was out on the links, playing a round of golf, squelching their way across the damp greens.

The club and golf course had been built on the site of a former wetlands area and bird sanctuary by a development company called Southern Pines. The boggy grounds had been drained and landscaped, then invested with a club building and restaurant, pro shop, swimming pool, tennis courts, and a sprawling eighteen-hole golf course.

Still, despite the extensive makeover, the ground was lowlands and inescapably tied to its marshy heritage. Beneath the spongy and expensive green turf, the ground was soft, moist, saturated. The greens always looked and felt as if they had just soaked up a day's rain. The roughs looked like wild thickets, no matter how often the groundskeepers cut down the brush. Water hazards resembled the Black Lagoon, with tendrils of pale green scum drifting on murky black-green waters.

But golf is golf, and the four duffers were men who could afford to be out on the links on Monday morning, when most workaday-world citizens were already toiling hard at their jobs.

Among the foursome was Dickie Thurman, an outwardly smooth operator, a golden (aging) boy. He was so suave, he wore both an ascot and a bowtie. His two-toned yellow-and-white shirt was color-coordinated with a pair of matching green-yellow-and-white plaid pants. White golf shoes with feathered fan-shaped white tongues, and a flat over-sized, green-and-white checked golf cap with a yellow pom-pom, completed his ensemble.

It was the kind of outfit that no man would dare wear anywhere on the planet besides the golf course. And not many would wear it there, either. But self-consciousness was alien to Dickie's internal makeup.

The quartet was on the putting green. One of them was taking a run at a ten-foot putt.

A cloud of gnats buzzed around him while he tried to line the putt up. He waved a hand in front of his face, trying to disperse the bugs.

He putted, his ball rolling four feet past the cup.

In a grotesque parody of Desi Arnaz, Dickie said, "Lucy, you got some 'splainin' to do."

The guy who'd just missed the putt gave him a dirty look. He rubbed his mouth and nose, as if wiping something off. "These damned bugs, they're everywhere!"

He took up a stance over the ball, weighing the shot, sizing it up. Just as he was getting into his concentration, he was startled by the trilling of Dickie's cell phone.

Smiling frostily at the other, Dickie unclipped the phone from his belt, flipping it open into readiness, too cool. "Yeah?"

At the other end of the connection, Irene said, "You're an asshole!"

Not immediately recognizing the voice, Dickie was temporarily stumped. Any number of females of his acquaintance might well have chosen to call him to deliver such a message.

He said, "Huh? Who is this?"

"It's your mother. I've invented a time machine so I can go back to the first trimester and pull you out with a hanger."

Now he knew who it was. "Oh, hi, Irene. What's new?"

She was steamed. "Don't give me that innocent crap. I'm in a police station somewhere in Rhode Island, and they're shipping me back up to Messina for some bogus hit-and-run charge."

"What the . . . ?" Always complications, Dickie said to himself. "Slow down, Irene. I don't know what in God in heaven's name you're talking about."

She wasn't buying. "Cut the act, Dickie. I know you're somehow behind this."

"I'm being a straight-shooter here. Now if you want help, I'll help," he said. "Just give me all the details so I can get to the bottom of this."

The other guy putted, sinking his putt. When he reached into the cup to retrieve his ball, a frog jumped out, scaring the hell out of him.

At the station, Captain Partington wouldn't let Charlie go on duty, telling him to go home. Charlie was crestfallen, woeful. The captain tried to cheer him up by telling him he had an important job for him to do, no mere make-work but a genuine official assignment, one that would take a day or two to carry out. So Charlie should go home and rest up for the big day tomorrow.

At home, Charlie told the brood that he would be away tomorrow and probably most of the day after that, on a prisoner transport mission.

The homies at-home were less than happy. Looking dubious, Lee Harvey said, "Messina, New York? That's damn near Canada."

Charlie said, "I know, I know, it wasn't my idea. I've got to escort this gal up there, then the captain ordered me to start a week vacation."

Shonte Jr. said, "Why a week, Daddy? That's a long motherfuckin' time."

Charlie smiled weakly, with his lips closed. "Well, he wants me to relax some while I'm getting used to this medication."

Jamal stepped forward, putting a hand on Charlie's shoulder. "Well, don't worry about us, Daddy. We all growed up now."

"Yes, you are," Charlie said, getting a little choked up.

"One of these muttonheads can do the shopping and I'll do the cooking."

"That sounds good."

Lee Harvey said, "You do the cooking? Shit. Ain't you the one who thought you got chipped beef from a toofy blowjob? You'll have Shonte Jr. looking like that Sally McBeal bitch."

Shonte Jr. said feelingly, "Someone give that girl a sammitch, I'll tell you what."

Jamal said, "She the poster girl for a famine-relief ad."

Charlie's smile widened. Then he remembered his parental duties, and spoke seriously to the lads. "Now, you know the house rules—no bitches after eleven."

Inside the main building at the Mississaugua Country Club, a cocktail party was in progress. There were light, brightness, attractive, affluent people of both sexes, some even socializing with their own spouses.

There was the merry tinkle of ice cubes rattling against drink glasses and the murmuring rise and fall of conventional conversational banalities.

Most of all, there was booze.

Dickie Thurman could use another drink, and he had business to take care of. Nothing unusual there. Lots of business deals got started at the club, out on the links, or over cocktails in the clubhouse.

His business required that he be out of the clubhouse. Turning his back on all the light and glitter and festive partygoers, Dickie crossed the expanse of melon-colored waxed wooden floor, making his way toward the veranda.

A sliding screen door stood behind him and the exterior. He opened it, letting a horde of flying insects into the clubhouse. He shut the screen door behind him.

The verandah was a rounded shelf of paved flagstones, interrupted by a half dozen or so scattered round tables with white iron lawn chairs grouped around them, the tables sprouting upright umbrella poles whose shades were now folded in for the night, like reefed sails.

Colored globe lights were strung on wires over the patio, providing a checkerboard of squares of intimate yellow light intermixed with shadow.

Overpowering all, though, was a weird electrical device, a square-sided upright rectangular screened-in box, emitting an eerie purple light, humming like a transformer.

It was a bug zapper, and every few seconds another sparking *zzzzt!* sounded as another insect rushed flying to its own destruction, zapped by the zapper. It crackled nearly continuously, so that a kind of toasty smell hovered over the damp stones of the patio.

The patio was mostly deserted, except for one or two adulterous couples who lurked in the shadows, even less desirious of notice than was Dickie Thurman. He went as far away as he could from the zapper, to a quiet corner at the far end of the patio, opposite the clubhouse's glass wall.

Beyond the zone of light lay the dark, moist grounds of the golf course, the air thick with swarms of gnats. From the darkened grounds near the water hazard came a constant rustling and unnerving hissing, the sound of interloping geese jousting among the marshy reeds.

A figure materialized out of the shadows, appearing beside Dickie. There was nothing ghostly about this figure, which was plenty material. It was Joe Gerke, a big guy with a seamed weathered face and narrow slitted eyes, dressed in casual sport clothes. His off-the-rack jacket could not disguise the bulge of a firearm hidden below it, worn somewhere on his waistband.

Irked, petulant, Dickie said, "What took you so long?"

Gerke said easily, "Hey, I came soon as I could. You know it don't look good for me being here."

Dickie waved away the other's concerns with a hand, dismissing them. "Yeah, yeah."

Dickie was glum. Mistakes had been made. Now they had to be unmade. "What'd you find out?"

"Got a few things," Gerke said. "Who the hell is this Irene honey anyway?"

"She worked for me the past couple years. I liked her. She was ditsy, but she wasn't stupid, you know?"

Gerke had his own ideas as to who the stupid one was, but he kept them to himself. "How inside did she get?"

"Hard to say. I hired her to be the golf course superintendent. This gal was a whiz kid, graduated top of her class. Turned out she didn't know squat about starting up a golf course. I had to hold her hand, lay seed with her. Anyway, we got close— you know how it is, the little head got hard and the big one got soft. I tried to keep her out of the negotiations, but she may have gotten wind of things."

Now it had been said. Gerke had done enough of these types of things before to know that most people were so afraid of the facts of life that they didn't even like to admit them to themselves. They had to be led to it gradually, until they saw that for certain problems, there was only one solution.

He'd work up to it, it was early yet. For now, he tightened the screws a little more on the other one, giving him a reality check, big-time.

Gerke said disgustedly, "For the love of shit.

These are the loose ends that can hang you, Dickie—and me, too. Why'd you let her leave?"

Dickie shrugged. The truth was that whatever he and Irene had once had, had gone sour, until at the end he couldn't wait to be rid of the ballbreaker.

He said, "It was, ah, complicated. I thought she was making things easy by blowing town. Now this hit-and-run shit pops up, and I'm wondering if maybe I was too sentimental."

"Well, we're gonna find out. The complaint was signed by a guy named Peterson."

"Never heard of him."

Gerke dropped the bombshell. "He's with the EPA."

Dickie turned his head, looking sharply at the other. "EPA? I thought they were in our pocket."

Gerke grunted. "Not all of 'em."

Dickie frowned. This was not good.

The bug zapper flickered and sparked like purple spring lightning. By the dark pond, unseen geese hissed, clashing, wings fluttering.

Chapter Three

CHARLIE WAS SUITED UP IN FULL RHODE ISLAND
State Police trooper regalia, as required for an official representative of the department engaged on a
mission to another law enforcement agency. Shortly
after nine o'clock Tuesday morning, having completed his round of preventive maintenance on his
motorcycle, he made ready to transport his prisoner
to the New York State Police station at Messina,
New York.

He stuffed his carry bag into the side compartment of his police motorcycle. Captain Partington
and Irene stood nearby, Irene holding a motorcycle
helmet by the strap.

She said, "When you said you'd give me a ride
back to Messina, I thought you meant by car."

Partington looked sideways at her, his face
neutral. "I wish we had one we could spare, Miss
Waters. The department is underfunded and undere-
quipped. We just don't have an extra car we can

be without for that long. But Charlie Baileygates is one of our best motorcycle troopers. He'll get you there, no fear of that."

The captain looked around. "Nice day, too, so you won't have to worry about getting rained on. Motorcycle riding can be treacherous on rain-slick pavement. Why, you wouldn't believe some of the bike accidents I've seen. You couldn't get me on one of those things—! But you're young. For you, it'll be an adventure."

Unenthusiastic, Irene put on the helmet she'd been supplied with, tucking her hair up inside it and out of the way, fastening the chin strap.

The captain walked her over to the motorcycle. He handed Charlie a manila envelope, containing the paperwork for the prisoner transfer. Charlie put it away, then mounted the motorcycle, kick-starting the big-ass engine into life, the exhaust making vrooming sounds, the machine shuddering.

Irene climbed on the back, perched stiffly upright on the seat. Charlie said, "Just hang on, ma'am."

Irene held on to the seat. Charlie worked clutch and throttle and the machine started forward, swinging around the barracks parking lot and making for the driveway connecting it with the highway.

Maryann stood near the door, watching Charlie and his official charge bike onto the highway and away, out of sight.

She said, "This vacation is just what Charlie needs. I bet he's a new man when he gets back."

Partington said gruffly, "If we let him back."

Maryann, alarmed, asked, "What do you mean?"

"I mean he's becoming too big of a liability. We may have to let him go."

"But, Captain, police work is Charlie's whole—"

"I know, dammit," the captain said sadly. "I know."

Charlie and Irene, those uneasy riders, set off by chopper to discover America, or at least that part of it that lay between Rhode Island and Messina, New York. Going west, they found suburbs, strip malls, and highways. The towns became few and far between, with patches of woods and fields stretching between them. Soon even the roadside food-and-fuel stops became few and far between.

In upstate New York, the landscape featured pine forests interspersed with clear farmlands. The air was crisp and clear. Irene, bored, clung to her seat behind Charlie, while the motorcycle zoomed along the highway.

They stopped at a gas station, the police bike halting beside a pump. In the center of the pump island was a small square clear Plexiglas booth with a male attendant seated inside. He stayed inside, not moving.

It was a self-serve station. Charlie unscrewed the gas cap and stuck a nozzle in it, pumping octane, fuel gurgling in the tank.

Irene got off the bike, stretching. She went toward a soda machine.

Charlie finished filling the tank and hung the nozzle back in its place on the gas pump. Helmet held under one arm, Charlie went to the Plexiglas booth. The attendant within was a round-faced, double-chinned young guy with pimples and blank button eyes, wearing a duckbilled red baseball cap and matching jumpsuit, emblazoned with the gas company's logo.

Also inside the booth were cigarette boxes and packs, Slim-Jims, tree-shaped air fresheners, chewing gum, and similar items. Gauges showed how many gallons of gas each individual pump was dispensing.

Charlie slid a twenty-dollar bill under the small opening in the front of the Plexiglas booth. "That's for the gas, and I'll take a pack of Tums, please and thank you."

Speaking through a built-in microphone that made his voice sound as if it were humming through a kazoo, the attendant said, "No Tums."

"Oh, that is a disappointment."

The attendant stared at Charlie, blinking a couple of times. Charlie said, "I'll need a receipt, please." He checked the total of the receipt carefully, before putting it away in his wallet. This was official trooper record-keeping. If he failed to properly account for his expenses along the way with the correct receipts, he'd have to make up the difference out of his own pocket. Charlie was scrupulously diligent about such things.

He went over to the motorcycle, where Irene stood, drinking from a bottle of juice. She handed him a fresh, unopened bottle, saying, "Here. Drink this."

He took it, eyeing the label. "Papaya?"

"It's good for the belly."

Charlie opened the juice and drank some. For a moment, neither he nor Irene spoke. When he'd drunk half the bottle, Charlie said, "By the way, um . . . I'm really sorry about all this. I wish we could've handled the whole thing from Rhode Island—it would've been easier for everyone."

Irene said, tight-lipped, "Mm." After a pause, her mouth softened, and she looked not so much hostile as resigned. "I suppose it's my own fault."

"What happened—you didn't see the guy?"

"I told you, there wasn't any accident," she said. "I just let myself get involved with the wrong person."

"What do you mean?"

"A guy. You know, we had a . . . it's a long story."

She looked so unhappy, that Charlie was moved to comfort her, awkwardly patting her on the back. "You don't have to explain. I've been there . . . I mean, with a girl."

She straightened up, squaring her shoulders, her

chin upthrust. Defiantly she said, "Well, I'll never be there again."

Her lips were firm, but her eyes moistened. Looking away, she put her helmet back on. Not wanting to intrude on her privacy, Charlie crossed to a trash barrel, tossing in his empty juice bottle. He couldn't be sure, but the agitations of his innards seemed to be subsiding. Maybe that papaya stuff was working after all.

On the other side of the concrete island, a car pulled away from the pumps, the driver throwing a bag of fast-food trash through the open passenger side window, aiming at the trashcan.

He missed, the bag bursting, spilling trash on the on the pavement. Speeding up, he took off out of the gas station, driving away down the highway.

Charlie sighed, then bent over, picking up the trash and dropping it in the can, along with other scraps that had missed their target.

Irene, irate, said, "Hey, you're a cop. You should arrest that asshole."

"Well, at least he aimed for the can. What am I gonna do, give him a ticket for trying? Anyway, we're out of Rhode Island, so I've got no jurisdiction here."

He finished picking up the trash. The unease in his belly, which the papaya juice had temporarily quelled, was once more flaring up.

He felt better later, farther down the road. Irene had her arms around his waist and was resting her sleepy helmeted head on his shoulder as they cruised along the highway. Charlie glanced at her, feeling pretty good after all.

Up ahead was a four-way intersection, with a sign reading MESSINA, 26 MILES. Not far beyond, the motorcycle slowed, exiting the freeway and entering a country road, a two-lane blacktop strip that rolled through a landscape of open fields and thickets of woods.

From time to time, they passed farms on either side of the road, with farmhouses, barns, silos, sheds, and outbuildings. The terrain was filled with rises, hollows, and blind curves, causing Charlie to slow down. Other vehicles were few and far between.

On an empty stretch, a thing lay motionless in the center of the road, sprawled across the white divider line, blocking the road on both sides. Charlie slowed, halting the bike within a few feet of the 300-plus-pound carcass.

Irene put a hand up to her mouth. "Oh, my God . . . it's dead. A dead cow."

That really steamed Charlie. "Damn truckers. You think they'd call someone to come clean it up."

They got off the bike, approaching the cow. Flies buzzed, swarming. In both directions, as far as the eye could see, the road was empty of all other traffic.

Getting a good whiff, Irene pinched her nose closed with two fingers. "Ewww. It really stinks."

Charlie said, "Yeah, by the looks of her she's been here a while."

Keeping the theme of cleaning up other people's messes going, good-guy Charlie hunkered down, grabbing the carcass by the neck and trying to move it. It was heavy, barely budging.

He said, "Well, it's gonna be pretty hard to move this thing, but we should try. Here, grab a horn."

Irene leaned over, pitching in, taking hold. Together, she and Charlie started to pull, hauling away at the dead weight, which suddenly moaned.

Shocked, they jumped back, alarmed. Irene, gasping, said, "Oh, my God!, The poor thing's still alive."

Charlie knew what had to be done. He shook his head sadly, his face set in grim lines. "You better step back. I'll handle this."

He loosened his holster flap, drawing his gun. Irene turned away, unable to watch, covering her ears with her hands.

Standing over the cow, Charlie tried hard to keep from getting choked up. "Well, girl, your suffering's over, fella."

He pointed his gun downward, firing. Irene jumped.

A heartbeat later, they both jumped, as the cow heaved a groaning *moo*.

Alarmed, Charlie fired three more shots into the cow.

There was another *moo*.

Charlie emptied the rest of his clip into the carcass, pumping out slugs. When he ran out of bullets, he turned his gun around in his hand and started pistol-whipping the cow with the butt of the weapon.

Moo.

Running out of options, Charlie put the wounded cow into a choke hold, wrestling it, covering the beast's mouth and nostrils with his hands.

Finally, mercifully, the struggle ended.

To hell with moving the damned thing, traffic could drive around it. Subdued, somber, Charlie and Irene got back on the bike. Charlie buckled his helmet, preparing to pull out.

Irene grabbed his shoulder. "Charlie, look!"

Still animate, the haggard, hard-luck cow struggled to get back on its four feet.

"Don't worry, that's just nerves," Charlie said, quickly peeling off.

The motorcycle went over a rise and down the other side, leaving the beast behind them. Up ahead, in the oncoming lane, was a tractor piloted by a farmer-type in a baseball cap, plaid shirt, blue denim overalls, and thick-soled work boots. He rose in his seat, waving at Charlie. Charlie slowed, pulling the bike up alongside the tractor.

The farmer had a broad, seamed face, a pug nose, and a lopsided smile. He said, "Just want to warn you. My prize cow Daisy got out again. She loves laying down and sleeping in the road."

Charlie glanced back over his shoulder, meeting Irene's eyes. After locking gazes for an instant, they both looked away.

"We'll keep an eye peeled," Charlie hastily assured the farmer, wasting no time in putting distance between them and him.

Cross streets became more frequent, now with blinking traffic lights hanging suspended on cables over the intersections. The country road widened, becoming a four-lane thoroughfare. Now the intersections had stop-and-go traffic lights.

A metal signboard on the side of the road bore the logos and insignias of the Masons, the Shriners, the Knights of Columbus, the Optimists, the Rotarians, the Chamber of Commerce, and Dwight Tuckee's Hardware Store, which had actually paid for the sign.

Beyond the signboard lay the town of Messina.

The police station was a tan-gray stone building whose front entrance was flanked by a pair of black wrought-iron poles, topped by rounded globe lamps. A gloomy old building, whose inside front desk area actually had a dark wood raised desk, similar to a judge's bench, where the uniformed desk sergeant sat, screening all calls and comers.

Also present was potato-faced Messina Police Department Officer Stubie, who met Trooper Baileygates and Irene.

Stubie said, "Can I help you?"

Charlie showed him the official paperwork documenting the transfer. "I'm Officer Baileygates— Rhode Island State Police. I have your prisoner, Miss Irene Waters."

Stubie took the documents, glancing over the top

copy. "All right. I'll let 'em know you're here."

He turned, taking the paperwork with him, going deeper into the building, crossing the white-and-brown checkerboard lineoleum floor, disappearing into a back room.

During the long trip, Irene had recovered much of her self-possession and poise, but now that she was actually back in Messina, a prisoner about to be handed over to the local police, all her anxieties had returned. She was taut, wary, fidgeting.

Her attention was momentarily distracted when she saw Charlie take out one of his pills, go to the water cooler, and fill a paper cup with water.

She said, "What are those for?"

Charlie looked away, embarrassed. "I've got a stupid thing where I have to take a pill every six hours or I feel . . . funny. It's nothing really."

He swallowed the pill. Irene, interested, asked, "What's it called?"

"Advanced delusionary schizophrenia with involuntary narcissistic rage," he said. He held up a hand, palm out, a placating gesture. "Relax, it's just a fancy way of saying I don't deal well with confrontations."

Irene nodded. "Does your ass feel numb?"

"No, but it gives me unbelievable cottonmouth for about twenty minutes." Charlie held up the pills. "They say it's only temporary."

Irene said, "I meant from the ride."

"Oh." Charlie got it, then laughed.

Stubie returned from the back room, followed by two individuals in plain clothes, dark suits. Every inch of them, from the tops of their crop-haired heads to the oversized flat feet in black oxford shoes, said *cop*.

They came forward, one of them flashing a badge. He said, "Miss Waters, my name's Agent Peterson."

Indicating the other, he said, "This is my partner, Agent Boshane." Boshane nodded to Irene, acknowledging the intro. He had a wide head, seemingly wider than it was long.

Peterson had wispy, pale cornsilk hair, a wide, round ruddy face, and intent blueberry eyes. He said, "We're with the EPA Special Investigations."

Irene, mystified, said, "EPA? What'd I run over, a bald-headed eagle?"

Charlie stood there watching, mouth agape. Abruptly, he remembered to shut it. His lips felt gummy, sticking. His tongue was a leaden thing, mired in his mouth. He smacked his lips, making funny noises. Obscene-sounding noises. Disgusting noises.

Cottonmouth, the dreaded side-effect of his anti-Hank pills. His mouth felt like it was packed with peanut butter, old, stale peanut butter. No—clay.

Meanwhile, Boshane motioned to Irene, saying, "We'll explain everything, ma'am. Right now we're going to ask you to come along with us."

She evaded his grasp, staying put. She folded her

arms over her chest. "I have a better idea. Why don't you explain it to me right now?"

Charlie's cottonmouth lip-smackings got frantic, causing the others to turn and look at him. He clamped his jaws shut, nodding for them to continue.

Peterson turned back to Irene. "Ma'am, we put the hit-and-run charge on the wire in order to track you down."

Who could like the sound of that? Getting a little screechy, Irene said, "Track me down? For what?"

Just then, another police officer came out of his office, into the front area. He was high-ranking MPD brass, a lieutenant.

Lieutenant Gerke, Dickie Thurman's buddy and criminal cohort.

He said, "Agent Peterson, I want to remind you again, our station's at your disposal. You're more than welcome to use any of our interrogation rooms."

"We appreciate it, Lieutenant, but we're all set."

"Well, if there's anything at all I—"

Here Gerke broke off in astonishment, staring past Irene at something behind her. The others turned to see what he was looking at.

The object of all their attention now was Charlie, who stood around awkwardly, his mouth white and chalky, his lips stuck to his gums in a leering clown's mask.

He mumbled apologetically, "I've got to find a drink of water."

He went to the cooler and poured another cup of water. His gummy lips were stuck together and he had trouble opening them to take a drink. He held the edge of the cups against his mouth, splashing it on his lips, dribbling water down his chin to his chest.

But the liquid unsealed his lips, so he could pop them open and toss back the rest of the water. He drank another cup, then another.

He went to Stubie, taking the paperwork from him and handing a document to Peterson. "If you'll just sign this release form here, I'll be on my way."

Peterson signed the form. Charlie thanked him, taking the document, adding it to the pile of paperwork, putting it back in the envelope, putting the envelope away.

He started toward the exit and got halfway there before he stopped and turned, facing Irene. He said, "Good luck, Miss Waters. I hope everything turns out all right for you."

His sincerity helped her muster a smile. "Thanks, Charlie."

He spoke to the agents. "Fellas, if you need me for anything, I'll be staying at the Chucky Cheese Lodge and Miniature Golf Resort."

They gave him polite nods, already forgetting him.

Charlie's mouth suddenly went dry again. His stomach wasn't feeling too good, either.

He went out.

Chapter Four

GOVERNMENT AGENTS PETERSON AND BOSHANE had a pair of adjoining rooms at the Red Rock Motel, a lodging place located on the highway outside town. The building was fronted with some fake plastic sheeting designed to look like a row of old-fashioned log cabins. The fake wood drove the woodpeckers nuts.

The motel stood off by itself, edged by the highway and hemmed in by wood thickets and weedy fields. Trucks and cars thrummed back and forth along the roadway, putting on their lights as night fell.

On came the Red Rock Motel's red neon sign, sputtering and sizzling, bathing the parking lot and courtyard in glowing orange-red light.

Inside one of the agents' rooms, Peterson and Boshane were sweating Irene. They wouldn't have called it that, at least not to her face, but that's what it was. They'd been working on her since taking her into custody earlier that afternoon at the police station.

All strictly legal, of course. The agents questioned, blustered, wheedled, cajoled, and threatened. Irene knew her rights, she didn't have to speak to them, but what else was there to do, stuck in the motel room with those two clowns for hour after hour?

The agents had a problem, endemic to their trade. Theoretically, every law-abiding citizen has a duty to cooperate with law enforcement officers to bring criminals to justice. In reality, though, being a good citizen may be hazardous to one's health, especially with all those kill-crazy types running around loose out there, ready to blow away a witness with no more thought than they'd give to blowing their own noses.

Now, Peterson and Boshane were working on Irene, trying to turn her. The air was stale with cigarette smoke, sweat, cold coffee. Boshane had loosened his tie, a touch of informality that seemed somehow to irk the buttoned-down Peterson. Peterson didn't say anything about it openly, but when Boshane had first tugged some play into the cravat, Peterson had darted him a sharp look, as if to say, you should know better. Boshane had ignored him. The air was thick, Boshane was heavyset, and there was dampness under the arms of his suit jacket.

Tugging at his tie, loosening it some more, he leaned forward, over Irene, who sat in a wood-and-fabric chair at a small writing table, near the door and curtained front window.

He said, "Yeah, we knew our investigation was dead in the water if we couldn't enlist your cooperation."

Irene fumed, as much scared as angry, but determined to show only anger. "How dare you! This is like Russia, only worse—I haven't done a goddamn thing wrong and you know it."

Peterson smiled thinly, his upper lip so thin as to be almost invisible. "No? What about the marijuana roaches you left behind when you moved out of your apartment?"

Irene could hardly believe what she was hearing, it was so medieval. "So I smoke a little pot—what is that, a crime?"

Boshane cleared his throat, said, "Yes, ma'am, it is."

Peterson chimed in, "As is being an accessory to bribery, embezzlement, tax evasion, and racketeering."

Irene looked from one avid unsympathetic cop face to the other. "What are you talking about?"

The agents looked at each other, Peterson motioning for his partner to continue. Boshane said, "Does the name Dickie Thurman ring a bell?"

Clearly it did, from the way Irene's face tightened up like a fist. Peterson smiled down at her.

Boshane continued, "His company, Mississaugua

Limited, has been under a sealed grand jury investigation for eighteen months."

Irene said, "How does that make me an accessory? I laid some sod on Dickie's golf course, so what?"

Boshane smirked. Peterson said, "We have reason to believe it wasn't just the sod that got laid."

Boshane tsk-tsked, saying with real or feigned disapproval, "Peterson, watch yourself."

Irene realized it was time for at least a modified limited hand out. She began, "Look, I came down to do a job . . . and we got friendly. I knew there were some funny dealings going on—Dickie's family ran with a pretty tough crowd—but I never suspected anything criminal."

"Tough crowd?"

"His dad's friends with the Clintons."

The agents looked at each other. Boshane made a scribbled notation in his notepad.

Peterson kept on drilling. "A big operation like the Mississaugua Country Club—how'd you get the job?"

"The truth is I got it by default," Irene said. The funny thing was, that part of it was the truth, as far as she knew it. Which apparently was far from enough, considering her present circumstances.

She said, "There was a guy named Tedeschi or Tedescho who was hired before me; he died—heart problem or something. Now can I get out of here?"

Peterson had applied the pressure, now he moved

to close. "I want to remind you, Miss Waters, we're after Dickie Thurman, not you. However, if you choose not to cooperate, I promise we can make your life very uncomfortable."

Boshane placed a leather-bound, accountant-type ledger down on the table. Irene looked at it, then looked up at him. She said, "What's that?"

Boshane said, "We got ahold of Dickie Thurman's personal ledger. We're going to go over it line by line. We want you to tell us whatever you know about entries, names, codes—anything you think will help us."

No, the cops didn't want much. Not much. They wanted it all, like always.

Irene sighed. It was going to be a long night.

So thought Charlie Baileygates, in a different context, as he tried to settle in at his accommodations at the Chucky Cheese Motor Lodge and Miniature Golf Course. The lodgings were located along the same highway as the Red Rock Motel. Truly, the area was home to downmarket hostelries for the undiscriminating wayfarer.

That was Charlie. He picked up some groceries at a nearby store, figuring it would cost less than eating his meals at a restaurant. Besides, in the upset state his stomach was in, he'd be better off with the ultra-bland food he'd selected. He didn't much feel like going out and being with people, either.

The courtyard was brightly lit by the floodlights

in the minature golf course, which was open for business day and night. Charlie's bungalow was at the far end of the lot, opposite from the small front registration shack.

Outside the front door of his bungalow, Charlie surprised a couple of critters, big furry varmints with long hairless tails. They scampered away, scuttling into dark underbrush. Possums? Or maybe they were giant rats, living off the fat of their brother rodent, Chucky Cheese?

Charlie went into the room, setting the grocery bag down on the kitchenette corner. He looked around, vaguely depressed by the seedy surroundings. The bedsprings were shot, the mattress sagged, and the bedspead was threadbare, fraying.

The TV was so old, it only showed programs that had been cancelled years ago.

Charlie went to the kitchenette, unloading the grocery bag, hauling out a loaf of factory-denatured nutritional-zero white bread, 100 percent all-artificial manmade mystery meat cold cuts, a jar of Mayo-Nos vat-made mayonnaise, a watermelon, a box of Tums for dessert, and some other stuff.

He took off his jacket, an envelope flipping out from his inside breast pocket. He stooped, picking it up. It was the folder containing the paperwork for the prisoner transfer, including a computer printout of Irene's mugshot, complete with photographic full-face and profile shots, wherein she was accessorized with a long horizontal plate held below her chin, bearing the prisoner's booking process numbers.

Charlie looked at it from different angles for a while, before putting it down apart from the rest of the other papers in the folder. The printout lay face-up to one side of the counter top where he now stood idly, one hand resting on top of the watermelon.

The melon's glimmering mottled black-green surface was incredibly smooth and slick, and almost voluptuously rounded, swollen to bursting with sweet red meat and mouthwatering juices.

Lost in a reverie, Charlie turned on the propane stove and loaded the watermelon inside it, his thoughts light-years away, daydreaming of Irene.

Contrariwise, Irene's reality couldn't have been more cut-and-dried, more tied to the numbing gravity of fact after minute fact, as the agents took her through the entries in the ledger, one by one, explicating the facts, grinding them to near-microscopic powder, dulling Irene's wits with an onslaught of deadly-dull, mind-numbing facts.

On it went. Peterson was saying, "December 12, 1998, 22,300 dollars to a J. Pauling. Who's that?"

Irene had long since stopped bothering to try to stifle her yawns, so she just yawned in his face. In a hollow-eyed monotone, she said, "Environmental consultant from New York. He came in every few weeks to go over the wetland plans with Dickie. Very proper, businesslike."

Boshane now had his jacket off, his sleeves rolled

up, baring hairy, meaty forearms. He slid a photopraph across the table, trolling it under Irene's nose. He said, "This the man?"

She peered at it, bleary-eyed. "Yeah, that's him."

Still buttoned-down, Peterson had yet to unbend to the extent of even loosening his tie. Tapping a forefinger on the photo, he said, "His real name is David Lamson. He's a Washington lobbyist who happens to be very well connected with some bigwigs on the House Environmental Policy Committee."

Irene said, "Huh?"

Warming to the task of showing off how much he knew, Peterson continued. "Southern Pines needed approval to build on the wetlands in order to get the golf course off the ground, but when the Greenies heard about the marsh being developed, they filed an injunction. Southern Pines stood to lose millions of dollars if the plans got put on hold. That's when Dickie offered his friends in Washington a lot of incentive."

Boshane, once more smirking, said, "Which is about the time your predecessor Mr. Tedescho found out what was going on . . . and developed a fatal arrhythmia."

Irene stared at Boshane, then Peterson. She was starting to see the light. "You're saying that he didn't . . . ?"

Boshane said, "You know Dickie. What do you think?"

Irene sat back, distressed. She felt dizzy, a little woozy. She had trouble breathing, she was green around the edges, and she felt like she was maybe going to be sick.

She hopped up, out of her seat. "Excuse me. I have to use the bathroom."

She hurried into the bathroom. The agents exchanged glances, Peterson's patronizing, Boshane's amused.

From outside, a knock sounded at the door. Peterson and Boshane stiffened. Irene was still in the bathroom, behind a closed door, the water running.

Peterson put his hand on the butt of his holstered gun. Boshane drew his gun, leveling it as he crossed to the front of the room. Standing at the door, he peered through the peephole.

He grunted, relaxing, lowering the gun to his side. Grinning, he said, "Pizza kid. I was wondering when he'd get here, I called in our order over a half hour ago."

Peterson took his hand away from his gun. Boshane unlocked the door and started to open it, only to be rocked back on his heels, off-balance, as the door was shoved in hard from outside.

A ski-masked intruder burst into the room, wielding a big-caliber handgun. He clubbed Boshane in the head with it, beating him down to the floor with it and stepping over him, weapon leveled.

Peterson drew, but the other shot first, blasting the agent before his gun cleared the holster. The ski-masked killer wasn't crapping around with silencers, and the room thundered with a burst of quick hammering blasts.

The burst caught Peterson square in the chest, dropping him, killing him instantly.

The killer looked around. Boshane lay sprawled on his side on the floor, inert. Peterson was finished. The gunman prowled the room, holding his weapon in front of him like a dowsing rod, the barrel quivering in search of fresh prey, a search that swiftly and inexorably led to the closed bathroom door, behind which came the sound of running water.

The killer kicked it in, charging into the bathroom.

It was empty. Above the toilet in the wall was a small square window, which gaped wide open. The gunman eyed it dubiously. Even for a slight-built female, it would be a tight fit.

More promising was the shower stall, whose plastic curtains were drawn closed. But the plastic sheets were translucent and behind them lay the unmistakable outline of a human silhouette.

His ski-masked face that of a murderously intent gargoyle, he used the barrel of his gun to suddenly sweep aside the shower curtains.

Behind them lay not a female human target, but one of Peterson's gray suits, hanging from a towel rack to unwrinkle.

Otherwise, the stall was empty.

The killer said feelingly, "Son of a bitch!"

He went back to the window, shoving his gargoyle head out through it, into the night. Below lay an easy six-foot drop to a patch of bare ground, beyond which lay layers of brush through which the light could not reach.

Time was running out. He turned, making a quick exit out the bathroom door, across the floor of the room, away.

The killer was Gerke.

A half minute later, there was the sound of a car engine starting up in the parking lot, the whirring of tires spinning on gravel, followed by the machine zooming out onto the highway with a squeal of rubber biting pavement. The engine whined out into higher frequencies and ultimately inaudibility, as the murderer's car drove away.

In the bathroom, in the cabinet below the sink, the door slowly creaked open, revealing Irene huddled into a ball in the cramped space therein, her face and body stiff with stark terror.

Uncurling her limbs, she crawled out from under the sink cabinet, hyperventilating, shivering. Fear made her move as stiffly as an old woman, as she forced her leaden limbs forward, across the tiled floor to the bathroom door.

Beyond lay Peterson and Boshane, sprawled on the motel room floor, the scene looking like a tabloid crime photo. Peterson was bleeding big-time but that was okay, he didn't mind it a bit, not when he was so defunct.

Irene had heard but not seen the shooting, so for all she knew, both agents had been shot dead. She preferred not to join them.

She fled, but not before grabbing her shoulder bag. All her money was in it, and her makeup, too!

Chapter Five

Nightmare! that was what Irene was living, on her flight through nighttime Messina. But at least she was living, and that was something.

Where could she go for help? The cops? The local law was in tight with Dickie, who had his hooks placed throughout the department. She wouldn't know which of the cops to trust, and it would only take one to betray her.

Betrayal? She'd already been betrayed. The killer had been looking for her, and someone had told him where to find her.

There was one cop she could trust, though, because as an outsider he wasn't subject to Dickie Thurman's corrupting activities, plus he seemed like an honest cop. Dumb but honest.

Charlie Baileygates.

She'd heard him earlier, back at the station, telling Agents Peterson and Boshane where he'd be staying.

The Chucky Cheese Motel. She knew where it was. Getting there was another matter.

Back at the Red Rock, when she'd come out of the bathroom and seen the bodies on the floor, her only thought was to get away. She didn't know if the killer had really gone away, or if it was a trick, or if he was working with someone else who was lurking behind to tag her if she showed.

All she could think of was escape, putting distance between herself and the murder site. The police might already be there.

She continued onward. She'd left her coat behind, too, and it was chilly. She walked along the side of the highway, ducking behind trees or squatting down among the weeds for cover when she saw the glare of headlights approaching from either direction. Chucky Cheese was less than a half mile away from the Red Rock, but it took her a long time to get there, what with all that ducking and dodging and skulking along the back ways.

The lights of the lodge's magnificent eighteen-hole miniature golf course glowed in the night sky like a beacon, drawing Irene to it. When she reached the motel, though, she was momentarily stumped as to how to find Charlie.

She didn't want to go to the front desk in the registration building, to ask the night clerk which room was his. She planned to keep a low profile.

The question was answered when she saw Char-

lie's police motorcycle parked in the lot. Each parking slot was numbered with the guest's room
number. All Irene had to do was note the number of
the space where the motorcycle was parked, and then
find the same-numbered room to find Charlie.

Of course, there was always the chance, particularly with Charlie, that he'd parked in the wrong
space, but that was just a chance Irene would have
to take.

She came to what should be Charlie's room. She
hated to be standing out there on the paved walkway
fronting the row of rooms, in the full floodlight glare
of the lights, but there was nothing she could do
about it.

Through the edges of the curtain covering the
front window, she could see a few dim lights, but
mostly the room looked dark. She went to knock on
the door, taking hold of the doorknob to steady it
for a low-profile soft knock.

The knob turned under her hand. It was unlocked.

That was something that Charlie would do. She
eased open the door, quietly slipping inside, then
easing the door closed.

She stood just inside the door, back flattened
against the wall. It was good to be out of the light,
here in the thick gray-brown dimness. The front
room was dark, along with the kitchenette, but the
hall light was on, giving Irene enough light to see
by.

She crossed to the hall, light-footing it, making

exaggerated stealthy motions, gliding across the carpet, into a short narrow passageway, and through an open doorway into the room where Charlie slept.

He'd fallen asleep with the bedside night table lamp still on. He lay on his side, wrapped in the sheets and blankets, which he'd managed to wind around his limbs and torso through the restless movements, the tossings and turnings of his uneasy sleep.

Irene crept closer to the bed. Hadn't she heard somewhere that it was dangerous to awake someone too suddenly from their sleep? Especially when that someone was a cop like Charlie, who for all she knew slept with a gun under his pillow and might come up blasting if he was too suddenly surprised?

She resolved to shake him gradually from sleep, gently. "Charlie . . . ?"

As she reached for his shoulder, something on the bed caught her eye, causing her to stop short while she took a better look.

It was the computer printout of her booking record, complete with her full-face and profile mugshots. It lay propped up on a pillow beside's Charlie, as if he wanted to look at her as he fell asleep.

Irene's face softened, her eyes shining. Charlie was really a sweet guy.

Then she noticed a blue jar of lubricating petroleum jelly and a couple of wadded, sticky, balled-up tissue papers on the nightstand.

What a pervert!

She punched him hard in the shoulder. "Charlie, get up!"

He started from sleep, violently waking up, sitting straight up in bed, eyes bulging, neck cording, making confused, turbulent snortings and gruntings. "Whuh . . . ! Who is it?"

He knuckled his eyes, blinking sleep from them. He saw Irene. He did a double take, grabbing for her mugshot on the pillow.

He said, "I was, uh, just studying your file, trying to find a loophole for you."

She stood with her hands on hips. "Oh, yeah?"

She gestured toward the lubricant and the soiled tissues. He said innocently, "Did your lips get as chapped as mine from the ride down?"

He grabbed the bottle and smeared a dab of the stuff on his lips, rolling and smacking them.

Irene figured he had to be on the level, so she decided to unburden herself. "Charlie, I need your help. There was a shootout! The agents are dead!"

"*Dead*?!" Charlie jumped out of bed, alarmed. He was in his undershirt and boxer shorts, the tangled bedcovers wound around him like a boa.

Irene leaned forward, intense, taut. "They were after me, Charlie! This is Dickie's work, I know it!"

Charlie made pacifying gestures, which were somewhat hampered by the coils of sheets and blankets twisted around his arms. "Okay, calm down, you're safe now."

Irene wasn't listening. She'd seen the thing in the

bed. Up to now, it had been hidden behind him, screened from view by his body. Now, it was plainly exposed, for all to see.

Laying on its side was Charlie's bed partner—a watermelon.

Actually, half a watermelon. It had been cut in half, with a dick-sized hole carved out of the center of the juicy red meat.

Irene looked at him. More in sorrow than in anger, she said, "They never look as good in the morning, do they?"

Charlie shrugged pathetically.

He got dressed and started pacing the room, thinking hard. Irene said, "What are you going to do?"

Charlie was struck by what passed for inspiration. "We'll call the police."

"What?! You can't call them! Dickie's got those guys in his back pocket."

"But this isn't my jurisdiction. Look, Irene, you've been through a traumatic event, but let's not get paranoid—"

Charlie's obtuseness was not only maddening, it was dangerous. What would it take to get through to him?

Irene jumped up from where she was sitting. "This is serious shit, man! Now, I'll run out that door and fend for myself if I have to."

That he didn't want. He tried a conciliatory tone. "Okay, okay, don't do that. Give me a second to think."

She kept up the pressure. "You better think some-where else. This is the first place they'll look."

"Right." Caught up in the mood of urgency, Char-lie grabbed a sweater and his keys. Irene was already at the door, opening it a crack and looking outside.

"All clear," she said, motioning him to her. "C'mon, c'mon, let's go!"

She stepped outside and he followed her. It was chilly and mists were rising from the trees on the opposite side of the highway. Charlie fired up his chopper, Irene climbed aboard, and the machine zipped out of the parking lot, into the road, and was gone.

In his haste, Charlie had left a few things behind.

Like his gun.

And his pills.

Somewhere along the highways and roads of the Messina area, the fugitives came to a deserted rest stop. A dirt path rose into wooded hills about seventy-five feet back from the road, to a grassy hol-low screened by pine trees and equipped with a couple of picnic tables.

One of the motorcycle's virtues was its maneu-verability. Charlie biked up the dirt road, his head-light dark, climbing up into the picnic area. A line of pine trees screened the site from the view of the rest area.

Charlie and Irene spent the night there. A couple of times, Charlie tried stretching out on a picnic table top to get some shuteye, but it wasn't happening. It was cold and damp, and they dared not light a fire for fear of attracting notice. Mostly, he and Irene passed the long dark hours by sitting huddled around on the wooden benches, hugging themselves for warmth.

Long hours crawled before the darkness weakened, replaced by grayness in the east. The sun came up, revealing trees and weeds heavy with dew, blurred by thin drifting veils of mist.

Charlie went down to the rest area, making a couple of calls by pay phone. He tromped back up the hill, to the picnic area where Irene stood waiting, rubbing her hands together for warmth.

She said, "Well?"

Charlie grinned confidently, giving the thumbs-up sign. "It's in the bag."

They got on the motorcycle and rolled down the dirt road, out of the rest stop, and back onto the highway. A couple of miles down the road, they approached a concrete bridge spanning a shallow river.

Charlie took the exit before the bridge, turning right onto a ramp that wound down and around to a road running ran parallel to the riverbank. Charlie took it, biking away from the bridge.

Calling out to be heard over the engine noise, Irene said, "Where are we going?"

Charlie said, "You'll see."

She'd spent a fair amount of time in Messina— too much time, really, not even counting what had happened to her since being forcibly returned to the town—but she'd never been on this road before. It was off the beaten path. There wasn't much around except for the river on one side of the road, and an auto junkyard on the other side, about a hundred yards or so ahead.

The junkyard was bounded by a solid eight-foot-tall wooden fence, topped with barbed wire. Above the tops of the walls could be seen peaks of stacked auto hulks, crumpled car carcasses heaped high in various parts of the yard.

As they drew abreast of the junkyard, Charlie slowed, turning the motorcycle off the road and into the main drive leading to the site. The drive was made of gravel, ash, and cinders, and made crinkling sounds under the bike's two wheels.

The main gate was a pair of metal chain-link fence doors. The chained padlock had been undone, and the gates gaped open, inward.

Charlie rode through them, into the yard. There were no guards, no dogs, no security measures. And no wonder. The place was a dump.

Charlie slowed the bike, putt-putting along at a few miles per hour. He craned his neck, like he was looking for someone. Ahead was a long shedlike building, with corrugated tin walls and a collapsed roof, a structure that had been long abandoned.

Charlie drove around it, rounding the corner and entering a space behind the back of the building.

Parked there, waiting for them, was an unmarked police car, a big-ass forest-green Ford.

Standing beside it was its operator, Gerke, clad in a dark boxy suit and narrow-brim hat. He nodded in response to Charlie's waved greeting.

Irene looked sick, felt worse. "What the . . . ?"

Charlie spoke in a voice to be used on children or childish oldsters or touchy sorts who needed soothing. "Irene, take it easy. You were being irrational back there."

"Charlie . . . why?"

"Hey, when people are in danger you go to the cops. Period."

"You turned me in."

"I'm getting you the help you need, Irene."

Charlie pulled the motorcycle to a halt near the front of Gerke's car, facing it.

Gerke approached, smiling hugely. "Good work, Charlie."

Charlie climbed off the cycle, turning toward the police lieutenant. He said, "Sorry to have you meet me all the way out here, but the poor gal was a little paranoid. My kids are the same way: somewhere along the line they got the crazy notion that the cops are the bad guys and the—"

He probably would have gone on a lot longer in that same vein, but Gerke put a stop to it by suddenly pistol-whipping Charlie across the side of his head.

Clunk!

Charlie collapsed, accordioning, then sprawling full-length on the ground.

Gerke started toward Irene, reaching for her. "And Dickie told me you were street-smart. Why the hell would you run to this idiot?"

Charlie lay on flat on his back, not exactly unconscious, but used-up, played, dizzy. His head spun, a merry-go-round, out of control.

Somewhere in the basement of his mind, a hatch popped open, and in jack-in-the-box fashion, up sprang Hank.

Charlie was gone, Hank was in charge, and it is as Hank that we will now refer to the individual in the RISP trooper's outfit, minus standard gunbelt and sidearm (a serious offense according to departmental regulations), that sly-eyed, loose-jointed fellow who now sat up, sneering at Gerke.

Hank said, "Drop the gun, you dumbfuck. You're being videotaped."

Gerke started, looking around nervously. "What are you talking about?"

"I'm talking about the camera on my bike."

Gerke turned, to look at the bike. Hank threw a handful of dirt and gravel into the police lieutenant's eyes, blinding him for an instant. Gerke raised his hands, crying out. The gun flew from his fingers, landing a dozen feet away.

Hank got his feet under him, hopping up. He struck a boxing pose, fists held in classic one-two position, as he began circling Gerke, bobbing, weaving, taking the measure of the man, then lashing out with a flurry of jabs thrown at the other's head, body blows aimed at the other's torso, punching and counterpunching.

None of which came near Gerke, who had finally gotten the grit out of his eyes so he could see again. He saw Hank and lunged for him, grabbing him.

Gerke started beating the crap out of him, whaling into him, landing lefts and rights, combinations and permutations, whomping Hank, who countered by defensively serving as a punching bag to the other, thereby eventually tiring him out.

Gerke was still going strong a minute later, beating the crap out of Hank, when Irene came up behind him and clonked the police lieutenant good and hard on the back of his head with her motorcycle helmet.

Gerke's knees buckled and he folded, collapsing, hitting the ground, unconscious.

Hank staggered to his feet, his face filled with the marks of many punches, his body slammed and aching, his legs rubbery. Flashing a cocky grin, he overcame his weaving enough to remain standing on his feet.

Brushing himself off, he turned to Irene. "Good move. You may have just saved his life."

Hank really was a cocky bastard.

Smirking, strutting, he walked around Gerke, stretched out on the ground. By way of administering first aid to a wounded brother officer, he kicked

Gerke in the ribs, hard. Gerke didn't even grunt. He was out.

Hank rolled him over, face-up, then crouched beside him, reaching down into Gerke's front pocket to steal his pack of smokes.

He also adminstered first aid to Gerke's wallet, relieving it of the onerous burden of the weight of carrying a couple hundred bucks cash. Hank helpfully lightened the load.

He would have lifted Gerke's car keys, too, but he didn't have to. They'd been left in the ignition of the unmarked police car.

Hank said, "The motorcycle bit is cramping my style. I'm looking for muscular gas-guzzling big-car performance in a totally unaffordable and ecologically unsound vehicle that'll have you shouting, 'Zowie!' "

Irene stared at him. "What the hell are you talking about?!"

"Of course, all the girls wind up yelling 'Zowie!' after I've taken them for a ride," Hank said, leering.

He slid behind the wheel, reaching across the seat to open up the passenger side door, motioning to her, patting the seat beside him.

He said, "Park it over here, sin-doll."

She frowned at him, leaving his rubber-faced smirk diminished by not one iota. She climbed into the front seat of the car. Hank put it in gear and drove out the way they came, leaving Gerke behind, still sprawled flat on an ash heap.

A couple of miles later, feeling that they were at least temporarily in the clear, Irene unbended enough to inquire about the driver's state of mind, that is, Charlie's state of mind. But Charlie was off minding another state, leaving Hank in the driver's seat, mentally and corporeally.

Hank worked the wheel, smoking one of Gerke's cigarettes as the road rolled by.

Irene said, "You mind telling me what you were thinking back there?"

Hank shrugged, head bobbing slightly to some unheard rhythm of the road.

Irene tried again. "Calling that cop was unbelievably stupid."

He said, "You're preaching to the choir, sister."

She exploded. "Then what the hell did you do it for? I told you we couldn't—"

"Hey hey, hey . . . tweak the high-end on your emotional EQ, sweetbeak. The funky chicken was Charlie's dance. I'm a tango man myself."

Hank let go of the wheel, freeing his hands to do a weird, pantomimed tango gestures, all the while keeping time with rhythmic movements of his eyebrows, working them separately and together.

It was scary, especially when the unsteered car started sliding over toward the concrete highway divider. Hank put his hands on the wheel, correcting their course.

Irene said, her voice hushed, "What the hell are you talking about?"

Turning to her, looking like Jack Nicholson in *The Shining*, he said, "Honey, I'm Hank."

"Who?"

"Hank."

"And don't call me honey," she said.

It was a complicated concept, but Irene got enough of it to realize that she was driving around with a crazy man. She fussed until Hank pulled off the road at the next food-fuel swamp. They stood outside the car, which was parked off by itself, away from the main building.

Hank stood leaning against the car's front fender, chain-smoking as he told Irene the facts of life about his bipolar mentality.

Now it was Irene who was pacing nervously back and forth. At least while she was outside the car, she could always run.

But to where?

Better try to deal with the problem at hand. Hank paused in his recital, letting her think it over. Finally she said, "So what you're telling me is . . . you're not *Charlie*?"

"Look at your feet," Hank scoffed. "You see any toe tags? Come on, you've seen Charlie in action. The guy's like origami. He folds under pressure. A bench jockey. When the big game's on the line, he's busy riding the pine."

Irene frowned, trying to make sense of things.

"Wait a minute, let's go over this one more time—"

"It's very simple," Hank said, looking like the kind of televangelist who flips out and slays six with a butcher knife, smiling all the while. "Charlie's the mouse who got you into the maze. I'm the rat who knows where to find the cheese. Name's Hank."

He extended his hand. "Hank Evans . . . for little girls."

He took Irene's hand and tried to kiss it, but she yanked it away. She said, "So it's true, Charlie's a schizo."

Hank shrugged. "I wouldn't know. I stay outta his business, he stays outta mine."

Irene's head was spinning. If she wasn't careful, she'd be splitting off another personality, too. She went over to a nearby bench and sat down, resting her elbows on her knees and her chin in her hands.

She was too nervous to sit still and popped up and started pacing back and forth again.

Hank said, "Hey, just because I rock doesn't mean I'm made of stone. I feel your fear. It's coming through like static on my heart radio."

Irene was unconvinced about his sincerity. That he was schizo, yes. That she believed. But he also seemed patently phony, insincere. Hank was weasely.

Irene said, "Um, look, *Hank*, I appreciate your help and all, but I'm wondering if there's any way to get Charlie back out here—you know, just for a quick conference in English?"

That irked Hank, seeming to put his nose out of joint. He thrust his lower lip belligerently forward. "Oh yeah, that's doable. And while you're at it, why don't you climb that pole over there and take a big steaming piss on the power lines."

Irene said, "That's about the only shock I haven't had lately."

Hank kicked back, sliding into some of that oily patented insincerity. "Look, I'm not here to twist your niblets, I'm here to save your life. But if I'm going to do that, I'll need your total confidence."

Not replying directly to his remarks, Irene said, reluctantly, "Okay . . . so what are we going to do?"

Hank's voice held a note of bubbling mania. "The game's hide and seek, their turn to count. The plan is we go on the hush for a couple days, find a cabin off-road, pick up some supplies, and then we just stay in the shade until the heat cools down. Sounds good, candypants?"

Irene said seriously, "Don't call me that."

"All rightie."

She walked away, back to the car. Hank trailed her, making faces behind her back, silently mouthing, "*Candypants, candypants, candypants!*"

When she looked back, his face was carefully blank.

They drove around the outer Messina area, circling, keeping to the back roads. The unmarked police car's two-way radio crackled with messages from the police station's central dispatcher to its various units out on the road. The MPD were swamped with the 800-pound Big Gorilla crime of two murdered federal agents.

So far, no message alert had gone out on the police radio net regarding Gerke being waylaid or his car being stolen.

Hank said, "Gerke's probably still out cold, so he can't get on the horn to sound the alarm." He looked smug. "When I hit 'em, they stay hit!"

Staring at him in disbelief, Irene said, "I was the one who hit him and saved your sorry ass!"

"Sure, after I softened him up first," Hank said, dismissing her contribution with an airy wave of the hand.

Up ahead was a minimall, with a grocery store, dry cleaners, video rental, pizza place, liquor store, and even an adult bookstore. Hank pulled into the parking lot.

He said, "I'll do the shopping and you play look-out, bright eyes."

Irene was tired from the previous night's lack of sleep. After Hank left, she had trouble keeping her eyelids open. Her head bobbed, as she kept drifting off to sleep . . .

The sound of the car trunk being unlocked woke her up. Hank was loading a grocery bag in the trunk. He stowed it away, slamming down the lid.

He got into the car, sliding under the steering

wheel. "We're locked and loaded. I got enough stuff to hold us over for at least seventy-two hours."

Irene nodded. Hank slipped the key in the ignition, but before starting the car, he saw something that bugged him.

A couple of parking spaces away, grouped around a car, were four husky men, big burly construction worker types. They were on break. One of them, who stood a few paces apart from the others, took a last hit on a cigarette, then tossed the butt to the pavement, where it landed in a splash of orange sparks.

Hank reacted as if the other had just performed an act of public urination, saying to himself, under his breath, "Well, fuck my ozone . . ."

Irene said, "Huh?"

She thought he had seen some cops or something, but she looked around and didn't see any. Meanwhile, Hank hopped out of the car and marched up to the man who'd just tossed the cigarette.

The smoker's surprise at the sudden appearance of this incensed stranger getting into his face was compounded when Hank barked at him, "Hey, ringworm!"

The guy looked around, not even mad, sure that Hank was talking to someone else.

Hank promptly disabused him of that notion. "Yeah, I'm talking to you, you toxic waste of life."

Now that he had the other's attention, Hank delivered his message. "Are you gonna pick up that

butt or do I have to glue it to the end of my boot
and stick it into your big, fat, pimply A-hole?"

The big man hesitated, stymied, much as a pit bull
would if a chihuahua should suddenly started yip-
ping at it, baring its fangs, mainly out of sheer astonishment. That a pencil-necked geek like Hank should
come on so strong to a pumped-up heavyweight who
could obviously kick his ass went against the natural
order of things, leaving the smoker wary.

The smoker said, "Whoa, man, I don't want any
trouble. It's just a cigarette."

But of course, such a show of reasonability could
only further agitate Hank, who thought he had the
other guy on the run.

Making a fist, Hank shook it in the other's face.
"Yeah, and this is just a fist, but if I start throwing
it around it can leave one helluva mess. Let's
dance!"

Striking an absurd fighting stance, Hank started
circling the smoker, bobbing and weaving, shadow-
boxing.

Hank may have been floating like a butterfly, but
it was the other guy who could sting like a bee, as
the smoker proved when he reached into a pocket of
his quilted orange utility vest, pulled out a stun-gun,
and zapped Hank.

Hank froze statue-still, quivering from the blast
of electric current. The zapper sounded like radio
static turned up extra loud.

One good jolt, and Hank hit the pavement. The

electrical contact broken, he was no longer paralyzed, but was now free to hop and flop around on
the parking lot pavement like a fish out of water.

It had all happened so fast that Irene hadn't had
time to react. Now, she saw the smoker turn and
walk away from the spasming Hank. The big guy
went to his car, got a tire iron, and came back to
Hank.

Hopping out of the car, Irene said, "You! Guy!
Leave him alone, he's a schizo!"

Ignoring her, the guy began tenderizing Hank's
carcass with the tire iron.

Chapter Six

LIFE IS UNFAIR, AS MUCH FOR SCHIZOS AS ANYONE else. Hank had written a check of kick-ass, but it was Charlie who had to cash it.

Charlie's return was gradual, a transformational process. Hank was gone, hiding somewhere deep in Charlie's mind, licking his wounds and content to let Charlie once more take the driver's seat.

First there was a big blank curtain of pain. Then the pain somewhat lifted, curtains occasionally parting to allow Charlie a dazed, confused look at the world around him. Mostly, it looked like a hospital emergency room.

The painkilling drugs he'd been pumped full of also put him under, and he was a long time coming out of them. He came to. He was in motion, walking, being helped along by Irene, who moved alongside him.

He was bruised, limping. One of his arms was across Irene's shoulder, she was helping to prop him up, keeping him on his feet. His knees felt in constant danger of folding.

It was day, he and Irene proceeding along a concrete walkway that connected with a curbside pickup area. Behind lay the entrance of a small, neat, modern hospital building in the greater Messina area.

Irene was urging him along, half steering, half carrying him. His eyes came into focus and he said, ". . . Whuh?"

She gave him a quick glance. She looked worried. She said, "Don't worry, Hank. You're going to be okay."

Charlie, dazed, had trouble putting it together. "Hank . . . ? Who's Hank?"

"Oh, boy," Irene said, not necessarily enthusiastic. She looked at him again, no mere casual glance, but searching, probing. "Charlie, is that you?"

"Yeah, it's me. Why, what happened?"

"You were in a fight."

Standing at the curb, motor idling, was their car—that is, Gerke's car. Irene urged him toward it.

A breeze lifted her hair, blowing strands of it in Charlie's face. He sniffed, anticipating a sweet scent. Instead, his nose made whuffling noises, and all he could smell was the medicinal scent of gauze bandages and disinfectant.

Charlie became aware of something obstrusive banging against his side. Lifting his shirt, he saw a loop of thin plastic tubing coming out of his stomach.

Too dazed to feel alarm, he said, "What's this?"

"A catheter," Irene said. "The doctor said you can pull it out when there's no more blood in your urine."

"Oh. Good." It was okay with him. Everything was okay with him. Charlie was an ageeable fellow, not like some people. The painkillers helped, too.

Irene got the car's passenger side front door open, wrestling Charlie through it, into the car. She went around to the other side, got behind the wheel, and drove away.

The landscape went by in a blur while Charlie's head cleared. Somewhat. After a while, he said, "I'm really sorry you had to meet Hank, Miss Waters. I thought I was bad—that guy's got some serious problems."

Irene, noncommittal, said, "Well, at least he saved our lives."

Charlie frowned, not much liking it. He liked even less the nasty taste in his mouth. It was not so much a taste as a slimy, nasty film over his teeth and tongue.

"Hey, what is that taste?" Charlie smacked his lips, swallowing, unable to shake the taint. The awful truth came to him in a flash. "Was he . . . smoking?"

Irene nodded. "Uh-huh."

Charlie made a face, then winced. Making faces hurt. So did not making them.

Irene added, "Anyway, Hank says we should find a cabin and hide out for a while."

"And you're going to listen to him? Look what he did to me—he's out of control."

"No offense, Charlie, but he did have a plan, unlike you. You almost got me killed." Irene spoke flatly, without malice, stating the facts.

Charlie, hurt, said, "Well, I have a plan now. I say we find a different police department and tell them everything."

"That's no plan, that's just making the same mistake twice," Irene said. "We don't know how far Dickie's reach goes."

Charlie said, "I doubt it crosses state lines."

"Okay, even if we did find a department we can trust, they'd call in the feds. And they're the ones who almost got me killed in the first place."

Charlie thought that one over for a minute. "Okay. I think it's time we called the best law enforcement agency in the country."

She looked away from the road for an instant, giving him a curious sideglance. "The FBI?"

The FBI? That was a laugh. Charlie would have, except that it was too painful. "I said the *best.* The Rhode Island State Troopers."

Irene's interest was once more focused on the road ahead. Unimpressed, she said, "You don't think the feds have someone sitting up there bugging that call? They'd be on us in ten minutes."

Charlie was getting more than a wee bit irked.

"All right, so what was the genius's big plan?"

Irene said, "He said we should hide out until the heat's off."

Charlie sneered. "Yeah, and what about food, what about—?"

"He already picked up supplies. They're in the trunk."

"Well, isn't he the little mastermind."

Irene drove up into the hills, where the narrow road switchbacked up long ridges covered with wooded and grassy slopes.

She said, "There's some nice private hunting cabins up here. The season doesn't start for another month or so, so the cabins should be deserted."

Charlie said, "How do you know? Or was that another of Hank's brainstorms?"

"Hey, I lived in Messina, remember?" She'd spent a weekend in one of those cabins with Dickie Thurman, but she didn't care to elaborate on the topic.

At the top of the ridge was a plateau cut lengthwise by the road, with cabins placed on either side, the sites set well apart for privacy.

Irene cruised slowly along the ridge, looking for a likely spot. No other vehicles were on the road, they saw no other people. One or two of the cabins had vehicles parked alongside them.

She found what looked like a good hideout, a cabin set well back from the road, connected to it by a dirt road, the cabin partly hidden by a stand of trees.

The car rolled up it, taking Charlie across a torture track, as every lurching jounce and jolt of the machine climbing the dirt road hammered the xylophone of his aching bones with iron mallets of agony.

The ascent done, the car rolled up to the small, single-story cabin, its windows dark, its doors seemingly locked up tight.

A perfect hideout. Irene and Charlie got out of the car. Irene opened the trunk, where amid a bunch of other stuff stood the grocery bag Hank had deposited back at the minimall.

Charlie said, "These the supplies?"

"Uh-huh."

He reached for the bag, opening its top, looking inside. Oddly, he was not surprised by what he found. Reaching inside, he pulled out a half-gallon bottle of rum, and an unusual adult novelty sex toy, namely, a fourteen-inch flesh-colored plastic dildo complete with built-in vibrator, which had no doubt been bought from the minimall's sex shop.

Irene's eyes bulged. Charlie said, "Well, he had a plan all right."

Irene, appalled, said, "That's it? That's all he got?!"

"Oh, no, there's more here," Charlie said, reaching into the trunk for the other items, holding them up. "A rope, a shovel, and a bag of lime."

*   *   *

So much for Plan A. Now for Plan B—if any.

The car came down from the hills, back to the highway. Charlie drove, having gotten some of his own back after the revelations of Hank's perfidy. Hank was trouble. Hank must be suppressed.

That was a problem.

Charlie said, "I'm not trying to bully you here, Irene, but I really think I should go back to the hotel to get my prescription."

"But that's insane!" Once the words were out of her mouth, Irene realized that her phraseology might be a bit controversial, considering the guy at the wheel was a split-personality schizo.

She tried again. "That's crazy! Er, uh, I mean, the place'll be crawling with cops."

Charlie said, "What's our alternative? Wait until Hank pops back out and puts your life at risk?"

Irene caught herself biting her nails, and stopped it. "Great. The only guy who can protect me from killers turns out to be a killer himself."

"Whoa, whoa, I am not a killer." Charlie pointed to himself. "He is."

Irene was not reassured. "Pull the car over. I'm not going back with you—it's suicide."

Charlie sighed. That homing instinct kept tugging at him like a pigeon called home to roost, or coop, or whatever the hell pigeons do when they're not flying.

He said, "Hey, what if we drive back to Rhode Island where we at least know we can trust people?"

Irene rolled her eyes. "But that's five hundred miles."

"Nine hundred using the route we'd take," Charlie said, his tone implying that it was a good thing. "They'll be looking for us on all the major highways, so we'll stay north, cut across Vermont, then zigzag our way back home."

Irene, thoughtful, gnawed her lip. It wasn't such a bad idea at that—but: "What about Hank? How are we going to keep him from coming back?"

Charlie pulled over at the next roadside pay phone. While Irene waited in the car, looking skeptical, Charlie got out to make the call. Security-locked to the pay phone stand was a local county telephone book. Charlie leafed through it, turning to the Yellow Pages, to the section marked "Pharmacies," where he used his pen to circle an entry.

Then he made a telephone call, to Rhode Island, to the office of Dr. Rabinowitz, the psychiatrist who'd been in charge of his treatment following the initial Hank episode.

It was during office hours, so with any luck she should be available to take the call. And sure enough, she was and did. Usually, he had to hold and wait for a minute or two, until the receptionist had put him through to the doctor, but today he got through right away, with no delays.

Charlie grinned. Maybe his luck was starting to improve after all. He was due for a break. Best not to get overconfident, he cautioned himself. He still was a long way off from having the bird in hand. So to speak.

Charlie said, "Hi, Dr. Rabinowitz, it's me, Charlie Baileygates."

"Oh, hello, Charlie," she said, sounding glad to be speaking with him. She said casually, "How are you making out on that medication?"

"Great, just super," he said, forcing a chipper enthusiasm he did not entirely feel. "In fact, that's why I'm calling. You see, I'm on vacation and I lost my prescription. I'm wondering if you could call in another one for me."

"That shouldn't be a problem. Do you have a pharmacy number?"

While Charlie gave her the name and number of a local pharmacy, reading it off from the Yellow Pages entry he'd circled, Dr. Rabinowitz carefully jotted it down.

She was watched intently by a team of federal agents filling her office, ringing her where she sat behind her desk, working the phone. The agents were all of a type, being fit, flat-eyed, and intent.

One of the crew wore a pair of headphones, monitoring the phone conversation while tending a laptop computer.

The conversation concluded, Charlie said goodbye, hanging up. Dr. Rabinowitz held a piece of paper on which she'd written the pharmacy number he'd given her. She hesitated, frowning. One of the agents said sternly, "It's for his own good, Doctor."

Dr. Rabinowitz, troubled, handed off the paper. "Here's the number."

The agent-in-charge read it aloud to the others. "402-555-7792."

The agent at the laptop computer input the number. After an eyeblink's delay, the matching address came up on the screen: HUNTER PHARMACY, CENTER LANE, PINEBOROUGH, NEW YORK.

"Bingo. We got it!"

The intelligence was presently communicated to the heads of the investigating team in the Messina area, made up of the EPA agent working the case on-scene, and his liasion with local law enforcement agencies.

In reality, this meant Agent Boshane and Lieutenant Gerke, who, along with Boshane's assistant, stood near a airport helipad, where a copter was warming up, its rotors whirling, its body thrumming with vibrations.

Boshane's narrow-brim hat was perched at a tilted angle, on top of the mass of winding, white-gauze bandages wrapping his cranium from the ears up. The hitman had given him a good crack on the noggin.

Gerke was no prize, either, sporting a square white bandage taped down on the back of his head where Irene had bopped him with the helmet. His face was covered with cuts and scrapes that he'd sustained from doing a face-first flop into the gravel after being knocked out.

The agent and the cop trotted toward the helicopter. They jogged crouching, stooped down, heads low, Boshane holding one hand on top of his head, holding his hat down on it. But he couldn't hold down too tightly, else it made his sore head hurt worse.

Boshane's assistant trotted alongside, giving him the latest poop. "They're in Pineborough, sir!"

Boshane said, "What's the estimated time of srrival?"

"Eighteen minutes, tops!"

As they neared the copter, the propwash blew off Boshane's hat. His assistant raced after it, retrieving it and bringing it back to his boss, who was now on board the copter, as was Gerke.

Boshane snatched back his hat.

The copter lofted.

Irene was off the part of the Messina turf that she knew, and Charlie didn't know it at all, and so somehow they took a wrong turn that put them on a country road while en route to Pineborough.

Irene said, "The good news is, I know we're near Pineborough. The bad news is, I don't know where it is."

The two-lane blacktop road wound through hilly farmlands. Occasional clusters of houses were found at the crossroads.

Ahead, on the right side of the road, a ramshackle house slouched on top of a rise. The weedy yard stretched down to the edge of the road, where the grounds were heaped high with what looked like household trash waiting to be picked up at the end of the week.

Nearing it, Charlie slowed the car. Seated on a lawn chair in the center of the bric-a-brac was what looked like Norman Bates's mother, an old lady in a straw gardening hat, faded print dress, and slippers.

Around her, there was all sorts of stuff, broken TVs, piles of record albums, cardboard boxes filled with old *Reader's Digests*, ugly lamps with torn shades, and a card table stacked with dented pots and pans. But it wasn't all good stuff, there was some junk, too.

Charlie pulled off to the side of the road, halting in front of her. Beneath the straw hat, she wore over-sized sunglasses, giving her sharp, pointy face the look of a bug-eyed praying mantis. A cigarette dangled from the corner of her mouth, clinging to her lower lip, a line of smoke rising from the lit end.

Irene rolled down the window and Charlie leaned across her, speaking to the old woman. "Excuse me, ma'am!"

She coughed, shaking loose ashes from her cigarette, sending them dribbling down the front of her dress. She coughed violently, hawking a thick glob of phlegm. "Hay fever."

Charlie said, "I was wondering if you could please give us directions to Hunter's Pharmacy?"

The old crone sat there, thinking it over, not moving, her expression turned stupid-sly. Stroking her whiskered chin, she said, "Well, that depends. You need any crab traps? They make great tables."

"Uh, no ma'am, I—"

"How about a set of Jarts? You can't get 'em anymore—steel-tipped, razor-sharp, these are the originals."

Charlie actually stopped to think it over. Irene said quickly, "Thank you, really, but we're in a bit of a rush here."

The crone took a deep drag off her butt, triggering a fresh round of bronchial hacking. Her withered frame heaved violently, spasming as she whooped and hawked. She coughed so hard that finally she coughed her false teeth clear out, ejecting them with violent force.

They fell in the dirt at her feet. She picked them up off the ground, wiped them off on a fold of her dress, then placed them back in her mouth, fitting them to liver-colored gums.

She turned her avid dark eyes on Irene. "Ya collect potholders?"

Charlie decided it was time to take a firm stand. In his best official trooper's voice, he said, "I'd appreciate it if you could just point us to Hunter's Pharmacy, ma'am."

The old monster violently heaved herself up to her feet, groaning and cursing, clutching the armrests of the garden chair. Her joints crackled like dried cornhusks.

"Goddamn tourists . . . y'all want everything for free," she muttered. Then, louder, began, "Okay, listen up. You go left down here at your first light, then . . ."

Following the old woman's directions, the unmarked sedan rolled down the road past the next intersection, a mile or two unrolling in silence. Irene said, "Look, I'm sorry if I was a little hard on you back there. I know you thought you were doing the right thing."

Charlie nodded, face blank. Irene said tentatively, "I suppose you must be going through a lot, too."

Charlie's lips quirked in a tremulous smile. "Ah. The good outweighs the bad with me."

Irene smiled back at him, fondly.

The area through which they were driving was one used by tourists for antiquing and leaf-peeping, with a number of roadside stands and vendors. One now came into view, manned by a Rasta in a hot-colored knit cap, the dreadlocked one selling bargain jewelry and trinkets from a card table, behind which he sat on a folding chair.

Irene frowned. "Something tells me we took a wrong turn."

Charlie pulled over, climbing out of the car and approaching the vendor. The sun was high and warm. He said, "Excuse me, am I anywhere near Hunter's Pharmacy?"

The vendor said, "No. You're going the exact opposite way. Hunter's Pharmacy is about eight miles back."

"Huh? But the lady said—"

Charlie got it. He'd been pranked. He frowned hard, scrunching up his forehead, squeezing out a drop of sweat that slid down the bridge of his nose, clung there for an instant to the tip, then finally fell off.

Before it hit the ground, Charlie was gone.

Hank had returned. Motioning casually to the jewelry and trinkets, he asked, "You engrave those things?"

A bit later, he got back into the car where Irene waited, turning it around and heading back the way they'd come.

Presently they came to the crone, who sat watching them approach. Hank pulled over, getting out of the car.

Irene said, "Charlie, what—?"

"I just want a little word with grandma," Hank said, flashing a bright smile. "Be right back."

He crossed the road, going to the crone. He stood over her, looking down. She tilted her head back, looking up at him through bubble-eyed dark sunglasses. She smiled nervously with her lipless lizard's mouth.

Hank said, "A funny thing happened to me on the way to Hunter's Pharmacy. Seems that when I came to the first light, I should've gone left, not right like you said."

Her smile trembled at the edges. "No . . . I'm fairly certain I said go *left* at the light."

"Well, my mistake then. I must've got on the no-brain train at malfunction junction." Hank's manic counterfeited good cheer would surely have unnerved a more perceptive soul, but the crone seemed to relax.

He said, "Anyway, I came back for the Jarts."

She nodded, dark eyes glinting behind the dust that filmed them. "Well, you're a smart man. You know you can't get them no more."

Hank lifted a suave-fucker eyebrow. "Oh?"

She nodded again, more vigorously. "The government has to stick their ass into everything. That's what Waco was about."

"Waco was about lawn darts?"

"Damn right. Once you cut through all the bullshit."

Hank pondered that one for a moment. "You seem like a pretty advanced unit. Tell you what, I'll make you an even trade."

Reaching into his pocket, he pulled out an item he'd bought from the roadside trinket vendor, a silvery necklace with a heart-shaped pendant. He held it in front of her, clutching it by the necklace, the chains and pendant coming out of the bottom of his fist, swaying hypnotically before her greedily glittering eyes.

Reaching for the bauble, she murmured, "My oh my . . ."

"Go ahead, put it on. You deserve it," Hank said. "Here, let me get that for you. Sometimes these tiny little catches can be tricky."

He stood behind her, fastening the necklace at the back of her wrinkled neck. The heart-shaped pendant lay flat on the top of her bony chest. Unknown to her, on its underside was the legend which Hank had had the roadside vendor engrave in a clear, concise inscription: DO NOT RESUSCITATE UNDER ANY CIRCUMSTANCES.

Hank reached down with two fingers, snagging her dented cigarette pack. She squawked, subsiding when he took out one and put it between her lips, returning the pack.

Taking out a matchbook, he fired one up, holding the flame to the end of her cigarette. "Here, darling, let me give you a light."

Instinctively she puffed, igniting the cigarette. Tendrils of tobacco smoke touched her lungs, setting off a fresh paroxysm of wracking coughs.

When they'd subsided, she settled back in her chair. " 'S'good."

Hank left, taking with him a fistful of the Jarts that he'd gathered up. Back in the car, he giggled to himself.

Irene said, "What's so funny?"

"Vengeance. It cracks me up," he said. He handed her the Jarts. "Here, put these in your bag, will you?"

He started up the car and drove away. A couple of miles down the road, this time on the right direction toward Pineborough, Hank said, "Got any smokes? I could sure use one."

That was the tip-off. Charlie didn't smoke. Irene, nervous, eyed the door, hand reaching for the door handle. She thought about jumping, but the car was moving awfully fast.

Keeping her voice even, level, she said very clearly and carefully, "Pull the car over, Hank. I want out."

"What are you talking about, sugar muff?" He put a hand on her shoulder, perhaps to comfort her.

She jumped, stifling a little shriek. "You stay away from me!"

"Whoa, whoa. What's the buzz? Tell me what's a-happening." He tilted his head toward her, studying her. Meanwhile the road kept on rushing at the car, curving while the car continued straight.

Not looking away from her, Hank worked the steering wheel, correcting course.

With dawning comprehension, he said, "Wait a second—You're not buying into Charlie's little smear campaign, are you? He's just trying to loosen the lugnuts on the Hankmobile."

Irene, vehement, said, "Yeah? Well, you were planning to kill me. I saw your so-called supplies."

Hank was crestfallen, sheepish. "Oh . . . that. Look, uh, I wasn't gonna just ram it home. I was gonna ease it in there, inch by inch, like a gentle-man." Shrugging weakly, he said, "You could even use it on me."

"I'm talking about the shovel and the lime!"

Hank didn't get that one for a moment. "Shovel and lime . . . ?"

Then he got it, or anyway he laughed like he did, doing a convulsive breakup. Catching his breath, he said, "I haven't laughed like that in a long time."

Irene, not laughing, had her arms folded across her chest. "Okay, well explain it then."

Speaking as if to a child, he elucidated. "We're riding in a hot carriage. Those sporting goods belonged to crooked cop Gerke. What do you suppose he was gonna do, take our dead bodies back to the station?"

Now it was Irene's turn to get it. "So, you mean . . . you weren't going to . . . ?"

He nodded sympathetically. "I know how you feel, Reenie. My radar's on and I'm tracking your blip. Now if you want to land safely, you better get your nose up, adjust your flaps, check you altimeter, and watch out for that windshear. Oil pressure's important, too."

She exploded. "What the hell are you talking about? Why don't you just speak English for once?"

"I'm just saying trust me. Everything will be fine, sweetseat."

"And that's another thing. I don't appreciate these nicknames you're calling me. It's demeaning."

"What are you talking about, honey hole?"

If he wasn't driving, she'd have punched him.

"Look, I think we should go to the pharmacy and get the pills."

"A-B-C-D-E-F-G-H-I-J-K-L-M-N-O-P-Q-R-S-T-U-V-W-X—why, baby?"

"Because A-B-C-D-E-F-G-H—I think it be safer to deal with someone who has a birth certificate."

He nodded amiably, conceding the point. "Well, I can't argue with that . . . but as long as we're mocking each other—"

He launched into a hateful, face-making mimicry of her. "I think it'd be safer to deal with someone who has a birth certificate."

Poised for her reply, so he could squelch that, too, he heard a sound from outside that caught his attention. Rolling down his window, tilting an ear toward it, he listened intently.

Irene said, "What is it?"

Ahead, over a ridge beyond which lay Pineborough, a helicopter suddenly bobbed up, lifting above it, showing itself above the ridgeline. It hovered, its tail turned toward the road on which the car drove.

Hank said, "Spark the radio."

Irene reached down under the dashboard, switching on the police-band radio.

"This is Unit 22. I have a visual on Hunter's Pharmacy. No sign of suspect's vehicle yet. Over."

Hank and Irene exchanged glances. At the next road, the car turned right, entering a narrow one-lane paved farm road hemmed by tall trees.

Irene said, "Think they saw us?"

"No," Hank said. "And they're not going to see us, either, my little scotch and soda."

Irene's face tightened, her eyes narrowing, suspicious. "Sounds like you've got another brainstorm."

"Indeed I do, doll." .

Irene sighed. "That's what I was afraid of."

Hank had the idea, but Irene had the geography. After he told her his scheme, she supplied directions to a place she knew outside Messina.

It was a long-abandoned rock quarry that had become flooded. Above it were cliffs, where the unmarked sedan now stood poised at the edge.

Hank and Irene had abandoned ship, with Irene toting a shoulder bag she'd filled with stuff she thought they might need before journey's end.

Standing near the edge, she looked down. About twenty-five feet below lay the surface of the quarry lake, colored a brightly metallic pale green, the still oval as slick and motionless as if it were enameled on the landscape.

No other humans or their habitations were in sight.

Irene said, "You sure about this?"

Hank had no doubts. "You kidding? Every oinker east of the Mississippi will be looking for this sled. Safer to go mass transit."

Irene nodded. They both were in place, and now they gave the vehicle a final heave, tipping it forward. The front wheels rolled beyond the cliff's edge, the sedan tilting down.

Horrible metallic screechings were produced as the underside of the car scraped against the lip of the cliff as it went over.

The rear wheels left the ground, the car's nose pointed straight downward, and the hulk plunged down into the lake, raising a tremendous splash that rose high, collapsed in on itself, and subsided into the lake surface, churned by ripplings and bubbles.

The car disappeared beneath the water. Irene said, "Good thinking."

"Think so, huh?" Hank's chest swelled with pride. "I appreciate the kudos. I'm glad we're finally on the same page."

"Me, too, Hank."

They shared a moment. Hank said, "I think you're a very special unit."

Irene said, "Thank you. That's nice."

"I hope we get to know each other better."

"Sure. That'd be good."

"You ever been pissed on?"

Irene gasped, then slapped him, a ringing slap that rocked his head, imprinting the outline of her hand redly on his swollen cheek.

He nodded. "I get it. We'll go slow."

Something occurred to him and he slapped his left front pants pocket. Whatever he sought, he did not find, and then began patting down all his pockets, squeezing them, turning them out in vain.

He said, "You didn't happen to pick up a wallet between the front seats?"

She glared at him, still furious.

He gestured lightly, brushing it off. "No problemo. It's handled."

He pulled off his shoes, toed the edge of the rocks, and dove down into the water. The lakestuff was so thick and opaque that there was no seeing what went on below the surface.

"Hank . . . ?"

Hank stayed under too long. Irene looked for him to resurface, but he did not appear.

She sighed, her shoulders slumping. She shook her head, the gesture saying do-you-believe-this-shit?

Straightening, she kicked off her shoes, standing at the cliff's edge looking down. Still no sign of Hank.

Irene dove in.

She broke the surface cleanly, engulfed by chill waters. It was still early in May and the quarry pond was cold. Underwater, there was slight visibility. She swam downward, stroking for the bottom.

Below, a ghostly outline took shape, the hulk of the automobile, which had come to rest upside-down on the pond's rocky bottom.

Inside was Hank, who'd gotten trapped inside the car and now bobbed around in it like a captive balloon, thrashing limply, head bumping against the inverted car floor.

Somehow Irene got hold of one of his arms and hauled him out from inside there. He was vaguely conscious, if that, and did not struggle as she struck for the surface, hauling him along with her.

Gasping for air, their heads burst free of the water's surface. Hank had swallowed a lot of water and now the stuff spewed from his nostrils and mouth in great jetting streams.

Irene got the crook of one arm under his chin and swam for the pond's edge, carrying the semiconscious Hank with her.

She hauled him and herself out of the pool, onto the rocks. Hank coughed and choked, long streamers of green snot hanging from his nostrils. But he was breathing under his own power.

Lucky for him, because Irene wasn't too minded to lock up with Hank for some mouth-to-mouth artificial respiration.

Irene sat crouched on the rocks, folded legs tucked to one side, palms pressing bare stone to hold her upper body up, while she heaved and panted for breath, winded. It took a long time before she was able to breathe naturally, in normal rhythm.

She and Hank lay collapsed side by side, utterly exhausted. Panting, she said, "What the hell is wrong with you?"

"I guess we can't swim." Hank spit up another jet of pea-green water, spewing.

When the spasm passed, he looked up at Irene. "You saved my life."

She said, "I guess that makes us even."

"Oh, no. I owe you."

Was that a good thing or not? She didn't know. She pulled herself to her feet and walked off.

Lose the car somewhere, in a place within walking distance of bus and rail lines. That was the plan. But they'd had to detour pretty far back into the boondocks to dump the car in the quarry pond, safe from the sight of pesky helicopters.

They stuck as much as possible to hiking trails and back roads, keeping a low profile. Hank and Irene were both tired, disheveled, and soaking wet. They trudged along, miserable.

After an hour or two, their clothes started to dry out. The clammy garments stank of pond water.

They came down from the hills, wandering a landscape of deep thickets and cool shadowy glens, eventually giving way to open fields and farm acres. They'd come a long way and had a longer way yet to go.

Out of sheer boredom, if nothing else, they resumed talking to each other. That is, Hank would have started chattering away long ago, if Irene hadn't kept telling him to shut up, cutting him off at the conversational pass.

When his later tentative remarks began to be met with monosyllabic grunts by Irene, he took that as a sign of encouragement, eventually breaking the ice.

He said, "So what's your tale, Mother Goose? Where you from?"

She said, "Everywhere."

"Hmm, omnipresence. I like that in a woman."

"Okay. I grew up in Texas—"

"They grow 'em big down there, don't they?" he said, ogling her breasts.

Ignoring him, she continued, "I came from a middle-class neighborhood, nice family, then after high school I moved to New York to—"

"Let me guess. Everyone in town told you you were easy on the eyes so you decided to become a supermodel, but when you got to the Big Apple they treated you like the worm, so you packed on a few pounds and started calling yourself an actress, but you can't go far with no talent and pretty soon the only bright lights you saw were the ones that hit you in the face when you opened the fridge.

"Then you got a boob job and started hanging around on the Upper East Side looking for some rich old man with a bum ticker and waved a white flag in the face of your own self-loathing.

"How's my aim, Mr. Lincoln?"

"Almost as good as your escape plan, Mr. Booth," Irene said, coolly unfazed. "I never lived in the Big Apple, I went upstate to Cornell, then got my masters in turf management at Umass-Amherst, and became a golf course superintendent." She grabbed her breasts. "And these are mine."

Not so easily fazed himself, Hank said, "I notice

you conveniently left out your eating disorder."

"I don't have a . . . Shut up!" Her face colored.

"Anything you say, slim."

"You know, guys like you burn my ass."

"But A-B-C-D-E-F-G-H-I-J-K—"

She held up her hand to silence him. "Because you're the kind of guy whose tongue is quicker than his brain, who doesn't have enough sense to stop and think before he says what's on his mind."

"Okay, maybe I do speak my mind," Hank said. "But if I don't tell you where I'm coming from, how am I ever gonna bone you?"

She made a fist to sock him, but was distracted by a throbbing pain in her head, the onset of another one of those headaches she'd been experiencing ever since the advent of Hank.

She rubbed her temples, trying to ease the strain.

Something in the near distance caught her attention. Below the grassy slope along which she and Hank slogged, lay a valley whose most prominent feature was a Ben and Jerry's ice cream–making plant.

Hank caught sight of what she was looking at, the ice cream factory. Its parking lot was filled with tourist busses and cars.

Eyes shrewdly narrowed and calculating, he stroked his chin, that feverish brain of his turning over plans and schemes. "Hey, wait a second, I know how we can get some money."

They went down the hill to the ice cream mill,

going among the throngs of tourists massed outside the building, who were either waiting to go on one of the guided tours of the plant, coming off one, or standing around eating ice cream cones.

Irene felt relieved to be among other people, strangers. Hank was intense, and being alone with him for so many hours was a trial.

Irene said, "Okay, now that we're here, what's your big money-making idea?"

Motioning her to follow him, Hank ducked around behind the back of a minivan, whose elephantine bulk screened them from the view of the other tourists.

He said, "Punch me."

"What?"

"Punch me in the face. I'll flag the big cheese and tell him I got rolled in the parking lot. They'll be only too happy to give me a wad of Benjamins. They don't want that kind of ink in family land." He smiled sweetly. "Go ahead and punch me."

Irene said, "Oh, I don't know, Hank."

"Come on, this'll work! But you gotta rock me. Don't give me one of those girly 'I'm afraid to break a fingernail' love taps. I want this guy to look at me and see—"

Irene tagged him with a roundhouse karate kick, standing on one leg, swinging the kicking leg in a blistering arc that brought the ball of her foot catching him square on the nose.

Hank somersaulted backward, collapsing to the pavement, a load of dead weight. *Lights out.*

. . . The lights came back again.

For Charlie.

Charlie looked around, bewildered, bloodshot eyes goggling. Barely conscious, he lay strapped to an emergency wheeled stretcher, which stood locked in place in the back of an ambulance.

There was a sense of speedy rushing motion, urgency, as the vehicle's siren wailed and its emergency lights flashed.

Charlie had already received some medical attention. Oxygen tubes were stuck up his nose, which was broken. His head was tilted at an unnatural angle, due to the whiplash-fighting neck brace that collared him.

Behind him, a paramedic studied a digital monitor, keeping tabs on Charlie's vital signs.

Irene knelt beside Charlie and made a cell phone call. Giddy with excitement, she said, "Hank, this is working. This is working!"

Groggily goggling at his predicament, Charlie moaned. "Oh, no, not again."

Irene got the message. "Charlie . . . ?"

"What . . . what happened?"

The glimmer returned to Irene's eyes, their black pupils swimming. "I've got Jerry on the phone. Just tell him you were mugged on his property and you're willing to settle."

She held the phone up to his face. Charlie mumbled into the mouthpiece, "Mugged . . . settle . . . property."

Click.

A dial tone hummed in Charlie's ear. Jerry had closed the connection.

The medical technician, who'd been keeping tabs on Charlie and Irene, now got suspicious that something wasn't right.

Leaning in, he said, "Do you have proof of insurance?"

Charlie said, "My card's in my wallet."

His wallet was in the car at the bottom of the quarry pond, but Charlie didn't know that yet. That was Hank's deal.

The ambulance stopped, unloading the devalued duo. The medical technician was decent about it, in his way. He let Charlie keep the neckbrace.

The ambulance drove away, leaving Charlie and Irene standing by the roadside, in the middle of nowhere.

It didn't take a genius to figure out that Charlie Baileygates was in trouble. Back home, his three sons were geniuses, so they had weightier matters to occupy their minds than the whereabouts of their dear old dad.

Lee Harvey was in a corner of the den, pumping iron. Jamal was interfacing with the computer.

Shonte Jr. was slumped in a cushioned armchair, reading a book.

Shonte Jr. frowned at something he read, then looked up. "How the hell can they call Pluto a planet? What motherfucking planet has an elliptical orbit? It don't make no sense!"

Lee Harvey sneered. "Sense? What the fuck you know about sense? You thought senate ratification was motherfuckin rodent trouble."

"Ain't it?" Jamal chimed in.

Shonte Jr. said, "Well, shit, Lee Harvey—you thought the Gulf War was between Titleist and Top-flite."

A message floated up on the computer screen. Jamal said, "Hey, check out this shit. Mo-though-fucker! That Vince Foster *was* murdered."

Lee Harvey scowled, not missing a rep in his weightlifting routine. "Would you quit hacking into them Pentagon files. Never mind who that horny-assed President be killing—just do your studying."

Shonte Jr. said, "Yeah, you know what Dad said about snooping."

Lee Harvey decided this was a time for truth. "You keep messing around, Jamal, you gonna get that scholarship to Yale took away. You be stuck over at Stanford with them slingblade motherfuckers."

The doorbell rang.

Lee Harvey said, "That's probably them Ivory League sumbitches right now." He was working out, and it would take an explosion to get Shonte Jr. off his fat ass, so Jamal logged off and went to answer the door.

On its other side was Captain Partington and a cold-eyed, blank-faced federal agent.

Partington, grave, said, "Jamal." He looked past him, at Shonte Jr. and Lee Harvey. "Fellas."

Jamal said, " 'S'appenin', Captain?"

"Um . . . we have a problem. Pack your bags."

Chapter Seven

A RAILROAD LINE WOUND THROUGH THE COUN-
tryside. Charlie and Irene followed it, walking alongside the tracks. Trees and bushes screened much of
the line from view of the roads, providing conceal-
ment, and hiking along the railroad right-of-way was
easier and more straightforward than thrashing
through the brush on thinly defined trails.

Even so, it was no picnic. Irene's shoulder bag
kept chafing her, forcing her to switch it from shoulder to shoulder. Charlie stumbled along, the rigid
neck brace giving his head a turtlelike aspect, as
though it was perched atop a turret and had to pon-
derously turn around to survey the scene.

His nose was like a squashed vegetable. It made
whuffling, whinny noises when he tried to breathe
through it. He felt gingerly around it with his fin-
gertips, exploring the outskirts of the damaged area.

His clothes had dried out, and were incredibly
wrinkled and rumpled. So were Irene's. They looked

like a pair of bums, two down-on-their-luck hoboes creeping along the railroad embankment.

It was afternoon and shadows were lengthening. Charlie touched too close to the injured area of his nose, producing fresh pain twinges. "Ow."

Irene said, "How's the nose feel?"

Charlie frowned, worried. He tilted his head back, flaring his nostrils. With his smashed nose, his face looked like that of a fruit bat's. He said, "Listen to it. It's still whistling. Have a look, will you?"

She squinted, peering up into his nostrils, not a particularly appealing angle of view. "Hmm, everything seems fine. I don't see . . ."

Then she did see it. "Oh wait, there it is. It's your septum. It's deviated." After a pause, she said, "Sorry."

Always looking on the bright side, Charlie said, "I'll get over it. Scars add character."

They resumed walking. She looked at him affectionately. "You've got a great way of looking at life, Charlie. That's a gift."

He shrugged. "I don't know if my shrinks would agree. They say that's what my problem is."

"What?"

"They say I purposely distort my perception to make my reality more palatable."

"Yeah," Irene said. "Like, you just hear what you want to hear."

Charlie ran his fingers through his hair, smiling

shyly. "Thanks. I like to keep it short, especially in the summer."

Irene gave him a look. "Maybe they're right, Charlie. Think about it. I broke your fucking nose. You should be furious."

"I know you didn't mean it."

"But I drop-kicked you square in the face."

"Hey, it happens."

They walked on. Irene said, "I don't know why I never ended up with an easygoing guy like you. That would've made my life a lot simpler."

Charlie said, "Ah, you ain't missing much."

Irene smiled. "I don't know, sometimes I think there must be something about my look that attracts assholes. Anytime a loudmouthed high-roller comes into the room, he makes a bee line straight for me. That's how I ended up with Dickie."

"That's crazy. You're a special girl, Irene—just look at you. You're just so down to earth. I mean, look at your hair. It's like you don't give a damn, you know."

Irene frowned, her smile dissolving. She fingered a strand of her hair, concerned.

Charlie went on, oblivious to her rising distress. "And your skin, it's so natural. You just let it hang out, blemishes and all. You're not afraid of your flaws."

Now she was depressed. Charlie said, "You got squinty eyes, and your face is all pursed up . . . like you just sucked on a lemon, but you pull it off."

Irene's hands were fists. "Can we talk about something else?"

"See. And you're humble, too."

From off in the distance came a faint hooting sound, the whistle of an approaching freight train. The grade was slightly inclined, the tracks following a wide looping path, forcing the oncoming train to slow down.

Irene and Charlie moved to the far side of the embankment, out of the train's way. With speed, power, and noise, the locomotive passed them, surging ahead, pulling a long line of freight cars behind it, some of them boxcars, others open flatbeds, the train's speed slowing still further as it snaked its way through the switchbacking gradient.

Inspiration struck Charlie, his eyes lighting up. "Hey! You thinking what I'm thinking?"

They had to shout to be heard over the train noise.

Irene, still bummed by his remarks, said, "I don't know—are you wondering how the fuck I can get away from you?"

It didn't register with Charlie, who said, "Quit joking. The train."

Irene gave him a look, hoping he was kidding. "You're not . . ."

"Yeah I am. And you are, too. Come on!"

Charlie started running alongside the train, his legs churning. He tried to turn his head, to glance back to see how Irene was keeping up with him, but the neckbrace got in his way, blocking him. He tore at it, pulling it off.

He looked back. Irene, hesitant, was jogging toward him.

Now they were both running. Irene said, "I don't think I can do it!"

Charlie, trotting along, gave her a pep talk. "Yes you can! Humans only use ten percent of their potential. You just have to reach down for that little something extra."

Irene speeded up, rising on her toes, racing past Charlie. He rushed after her, calling, "There you go . . . Now you're getting it . . . Don't you dare give up now."

A flatbed open car drew abreast of Irene, passing her. She grabbed hold of a rail handle, nimbly hauling herself up, her feet leaving the ground as she hoisted herself on to the bed of the rail car.

Charlie ran alongside the car, sucking wind, face red, cheeks huffing and puffing. Irene went to the rear of the car, bracing herself, reaching out her hand for him to grasp.

He reached for her hand, his arm stretching, fingers groping. Inches of empty air separated his hand from hers.

The gap widened, as Charlie ran out of breath, falling behind. His chest hammered, his limbs were leaden, there was a roaring in his ears that was not so much the noise of the train as it was the pounding of his own heartbeat.

The train drew ahead, taking Irene away from him. Charlie dropped back, gasping for breath, watching Irene dwindle in the fast-opening distance.

He called, "Jump!"

She couldn't hear him. "What?!"

"Jump off!"

"Huh?!"

He screamed, "Jump off the goddamn train!"

For an instant, as Charlie's form fell behind the long curving line of freight cars, Irene gave the proposition serious consideration, pro and con, and it wasn't just because the train was starting to pick up speed.

Reluctantly, Irene decided to jump. She stood crouched at the edge of the car, holding on to the railing. The ground rolled by in a blur. There was a grassy field with a lot of bushes and if she didn't make a move now it would be too late.

She jumped, hitting the ground with a hard thud, the impact muffled by the grassy weeds cushioning her, but not as much as she'd hoped, or liked. She rolled on the ground, tumbling, getting scratched and bruised before finally rolling to a stop in a cloud of dust.

She lay there a long time, then got up, groaning. She brushed herself off. Charlie was still a long way off, a manlike blur scuttling along the line toward her.

A few moments later, heaving for breath as

though about to hock up a lung, Charlie finally staggered up to Irene.

He crouched, gasping, hands on his knees. "Started thinking about it . . . Bad idea . . . Trains are stupid . . . first place they'll look."

She gave him a dirty look, but he was too busy trying to keep from falling over to notice it.

On they trudged, the hours lengthening, the day waning. In the late afternoon, the shadows long, the railroad turned away from the roads and towns, curving into a wooded wilderness. Charlie and Irene climbed down from the embankment, and once more began following the grid of country roads through sprawling farmlands.

Charlie was famished. His innards grumbled like a taxpayer on April fifteenth. Holding his belly, he complained, "My motherfuckin' stomach's starting to ache."

Irene glanced at him, brows knit, frowning. He said, "Pardon my French—I get that from my kids."

That confused her. While he'd been speaking, Charlie had noticed something, and now he confirmed it. "Hey, my nose. It stopped whistling."

Irene said, "Must've been a booger." Her spirits were in low gear.

Charlie pointed ahead, to a cluster of buildings at a crossroads in the near distance. "Look, a town."

They slogged toward it. Charlie said, "You got any dough at all?"

Irene said, "Six bucks."

"I have three."

That meant they ate. The small town's sole eatery was Ma's Homecooked Natural Foods Diner, sited near the highway. The parking lot was starting to fill up with cars, now that it was early dinner hour.

Charlie and Irene went in. The good food smells made Charlie's empty belly twist itself in knots, banging urgently against his backbone.

A hostess seated them in the back of the diner, way back, near the kitchen. Seated in the next booth opposite them were two mannish, crew-cut women, burly types in flannel shirts and wide-bottom overalls and Doc Martens. They'd finished eating and were lingering over coffee. They were smoking cigarettes. It was unclear if this was an officially designated smoking section, but no one cared to broach the issue with the two formidable femmes. They were pretty tough-looking.

In the booth behind Charlie and Irene sat a well-scrubbed family group of a daddy, a mommy, and a towheaded, freckle-faced, cute little six-year-old boy.

Charlie and Irene had been seated for a long time, without so much as a waitress popping back to hand them a couple of menus. Irene rose, sliding out from the booth to stand in the aisle.

She said, "Let me go up and order so we can get back on the road."

Charlie said, "I'll have a chicken breast sandwich, no skin, on toast—dry."

Irene went forward, going to the lunch counter. Charlie sat back, looking around the restaurant. Something flickered in the corner of his eye, catching his attention. Behind him, the kid at the next table was hanging over the back of his chair, turning to stare at Charlie while simultaneously sucking on a vanilla milkshake through a straw.

Charlie smiled at him. The six-year-old kept staring.

Charlie glanced back over his shoulder, trying to see if maybe the kid was looking at something else, but no.

Him. The kid was looking at him and no other. Not looking, staring. Gawking.

Charlie turned back around at the table, facing front. A busboy had left a couple of glasses of water and place settings at the table. Charlie picked up a glass of water, pressing its cool damp side against his feverish forehead, before finally taking a few swallows of the stuff.

He tried to get the gaping kid out of his head, but he couldn't. He could feel the kid's unblinking eyes drilling holes in the back of his head, like lasers.

Funny how a little thing like that could get under a fellow's skin. When you add up all that Charlie had undergone lately, including being worked over with a tire iron, having his nose smashed by a karate kick, and even losing his wallet, it was strange that a kid with reckless eyeballs was what was finally getting his goat.

Unable to stand it any longer, he turned around in his chair, thrusting his face pugnaciously forward, toward the kid, saying to him, "What're you staring at, fucker?"

The kid's eyes widened, becoming round, with all white ringing the pupils and irises. He dropped his shake, stunned.

That wasn't Charlie. Baileygates was a member of the RISP, representing a proud tradition he was duty-bound to uphold. More important, Charlie genuinely liked people. He would never, ever deliberately frighten or discomfort a child.

Hank would, though.

And did. Hank was back. This time, it hadn't taken any trauma, any blow to the head or similar violence. A lot of small things had added up and this was the last straw, the final indignity that tipped the scale, dropping Charlie down the hatch while Hank popped up in his jack-in-the-box way, taking over.

Charlie was weakening, losing his grip over the cockpit of his mind. Hank had the juice, the dynamism. Now, it looked like he had the momentum. As an identity-unit, Charlie was on the run and Hank was in the ascendant.

Hank was loose and swinging. Being Hank, there was a lot of resentment to unload, and brat-face was the lightning rod of his discontent.

Hank stood up, going over to the booth where the

kid sat and towering over him. He said, "You wanna start me up. Just open up the choke and pull the cord . . . I'm due for a seismic event and you're dancing on the fault line."

The kid was so scared that he pissed his pants. His mother was babbling something about Hank's being crazy, a crazy man.

Crazy?! Why, he was the sanest man alive!

The boy's father stood up, furious, but shorter and slighter than Hank. And don't think Hank hadn't taken in that fact, vectoring it somewhere into his calculations.

The defiant dad blustered, "What the hell is your problem, mister?!"

Hank airily waved him off. "Hey, I got no beef with you. This is between me and the kid."

About this time, Irene arrived, her stomach sinking with the sickening realization that the fracas could be caused by none other than her traveling companion, a hunch that of course was instantly proven correct.

She bit her lip. "Oh, no . . ."

The kid's father started to make a move toward Hank, but Irene got between them, intercepting him. She pulled the man aside.

"Look, I apologize for my friend but he suffers from, uh . . . he's got this uh . . ." Irene fell silent. What the hell did he suffer from?

She shrugged. "He's an ass."

The shook-up family exited, scrambling out of the

booth and storming out of the restaurant. At the door, the kid looked back.

Hank called, "Poor little baby needs daddy to fight his battles for him. CLUCK, CLUCK, CLUCK, CLUCK!"

The family went out. Everybody else in the place turned to look at Hank, their heads swiveling around in unison, as if activated by a single master switch.

"Pussy," Hank said, sneering as the door closed behind them. Irene, mortified, wished she could sink through the floor to escape. No such luck.

Leaning across the aisle, Hank reached over to the mannish women's table and shook a cigarette from the pack, taking it without asking.

He said, "How's it hangin', fellas?"

They just shrugged.

Irene said, "Hank, I presume?"

Hank exhaled, spewing a fan-shaped stream of smoke. "You miss me?"

"How about sending Charlie back out here—things were starting to get civilized."

Hank held up an index finger, pointing at the ceiling, with the air of one about to impart some deathless bit of wisdom. "Listen, Pocahontas, unless you keep your ear to the ground you'll never hear the buffalo coming."

Irene said, "I don't know what that means."

"It means either he has to come up with a battle plan or ol' Hank's gonna take over Fort Charlie for good."

Something he said weirded her out more than usual. She picked up on it, saying, "Excuse me, did you just refer to yourself in the third person?"

The waiter came with their order. He was a young guy, about twenty-one, young albino guy, with lanky white hair, white face and hands, and pinkish eyeballs. He started setting the plates of food down on the table.

Hank pointed at him. "Hey, it's a giant Q-Tip."

He laughed, a loud jackass bray. Irene was seriously thinking about crawling under the table to get away.

Hank said to the waiter, "I'm just kidding, man. Trying to bring some sunshine into your life. Careful, you'll peel."

He brayed again, heehawing. Straightening his face, becoming composed, serious, he asked with a show of concern, "By the way, they doing anything about that?"

"About what?"

"You know, the whole pink-eye, no-pigment thing. Any research being done?"

Thinking it over, the albino waiter said, "Well, um . . . not that I know of."

"Too bad. Makes sense though. There's no incentive—it's not like we're gonna catch it." Hank suddenly pulled his shirt over his mouth, covering it, wide eyes rolling. "Are we?"

The waiter shook his head, walking away.

Irene was furious. "That's it. We're out of here."

Hank said, "Hey . . . did I miss something?"

Irene turned on him. "Don't give me that shit. That was plain rude what you did to that kid. Didn't you see the look on his face?"

Hank's cocky smirk flattened at the edges, starting to implode. "He looked a little pale, that's all."

Irene said, "He was *offended*."

"Well, I don't agree, but why speculate." Hank gave two quick claps, signaling for the waiter. He called out, "Hey, Milky, get over here!"

Irene cringed, lowering her head as the waiter approached. Hank said, "Were you offended in any way by our social interaction?"

The waiter said, "Well . . . yeah, I was."

Hank thought about it. "What was it, the Q-Tip thing?"

"I was pretty much offended by everything you said, sir."

If the expression on his face was any gauge, this came as news to Hank. For a moment, he was at a loss for words. "Oh."

He cleared his throat. "Well, I'm sorry. I'm truly sorry."

Hank rose, walking away from the booth and out of the restaurant. Irene looked at the waiter and shrugged.

She got up and went after him. She found Hank outside, sitting on a bench, holding his head in his hands, dejected.

Irene said, "Are you all right?"

Hank looked woeful. "I don't know. I keep pitching, but I can't seem to hit the strike zone. I feel like I'm letting the team down."

"Well, you are, but . . . realizing it, is half the battle, Hank."

Hank looked away to hide his growing emotionalism. "You don't know what it was like . . . spending all those years locked behind a wall of politeness, bound and gagged in that dark and silent world where nothing grows but the anger. All because that doll-faced demon he married laced her boots up and did a Nancy Sinatra on him."

Irene said, "Charlie had a wife?" It did seem a little hard to believe.

"And then some," Hank said. His gaze turned inward, remembering. "I was a big piece of the personality pie back then, and when she left him, Charlie went numb and I went AWOL."

"Hank, if you were a big part of his personality, then she left you, too."

Hank thought about it for a moment, the import of it sinking in. His face swelled, scrunched up, his eyes squeezing out fat, oily tears.

He said, "It's true, it's true. She walked out on us. I loved her."

He looked up at Irene. "Why did she do this? I'm not a bad person."

She moved in closer, to comfort him. She put an arm around his heaving shoulders. She said, "I don't know why. I don't know. But you're not a bad person. You're a good person." She looked him right in the eye. "Do you hear me? You are a good person."

Hank stopped crying and began regaining some of his composure. "You really think so?"

"Yeah, I do now," Irene said. "In fact, I think this might be some kind of breakthrough."

Hank wiped his eyes. "Yeah, I feel good. I feel really good. You know what I'm gonna do? I'm gonna make it up to Charlie . . . and to that poor kid in there."

He went back into the diner, Irene following.

Inside, there was an emotionally vulnerable young albino waiter, seeking a few crumbs of respect and human dignity.

Plus there were a couple of uneaten sandwiches waiting, singing their siren song.

Chapter Eight

CHARLIE BAILEYGATES WAS A MENTAL CASE who'd flipped and turned killer, slaying Federal Agent Peterson and kidnapping Irene. That was the official view of the case, as detailed by Agent Boshane and Lieutenant Gerke to Charlie's three sons at the temporary police command post in the Pineborough area, where the young men had been brought.

They weren't buying. Staring at Boshane and Gerke like they were a pair of bugs, Jamal spoke truth to power. He said, "Dass boo-shit. My daddy ain't killed no one. And he sure as shit ain't gonna kidnap no skinny-ass bitch."

Agent Boshane smiled tolerantly. "Sure, you're going to stick up for Charlie. That's only natural. He's your dad. But Charlie's sick, mentally—some sort of breakdown, from what we understand. The important thing is that we find him before someone else gets hurt, including himself."

Shonte Jr took up the cause. "Okay, let's say he

did have a problem—which he don't—he been taking pills to get rid of it."

Boshane said, "He left the pills at his hotel."

Gerke said harshly, "And that's where he left his
sanity. I've seen it firsthand—the guy's nuttier than
squirrel turds."

The trio all stared at Gerke. Jamal said, "One
thing I don't understand, Lieutenant: If my daddy
such a scary-ass motherfucker, why'd you go alone
for?"

Shonte Jr. said, "Yeah. Who're you, some Lone
Ranger sumbitch?"

Gerke reddened, his pale eyes bulging angrily.
"Your 'father' is a police officer and he asked me to
come alone. How was I to know he's a nutcase?"

Boshane gestured to the other to ease up.
"Enough, Gerke."

Gerke rolled his eyes, but backed off. Boshane
faced the three youths. He said, "Anyway, you guys
know your father better than anyone. We were hoping you could help us track him down and end this
thing peacefully."

Gerke said, "We checked the major gas and food
stops along the interstate—no sign of them."

Silently scowling until this time, Lee Harvey now
spoke up. Still scowling, he said, "The interstate?
Let me axe you something: Is your old lady happy?"

Gerke reacted, bristling. "*My old lady*?"

"Yeah. 'Cause if your lovin' anything like your

police work, you couldn't find the G-spot on a twelve-pound pussy."

Gerke's face was heavy-lidded, sullen. "Watch your mouth."

Boshane, intrigued, said, "What are you getting at?"

Lee Harvey held up a hand, enumerating the points on his fingers. "A: Daddy ain't gonna take no road where your blind-ass Helen Keller cops are looking. And B: He ain't gonna eat no fast food."

"Why not?"

Shonte Jr. said, "Because he gots colitis. If he don't eat right, he'll shit like a Tijuana circus elephant."

Jamal said, "You got that right. That poor soul's had more cameras up his ass than Traci Lords."

Boshane said, "Well, that's something."

Up came Officer Stubie, red-faced, jiggling. Excited, he said, "Just got lucky. They were spotted leaving a backwoods café about a hundred miles northwest of here."

Lee Harvey folded thick arms across his muscular chest, smiling a mirthless self-satisfied smile. Boshane motioned to Gerke, the two of them moving off to one side to have a confab. From the way they were going at it for a moment, they had some strong disagreements as how to proceed.

A moment later, they returned, Gerke looking even more pissed off than usual. Boshane said,

"We'd like you guys to come along. You obviously know Charlie better than us."

Lee Harvey nodded. Boshane and Gerke turned, going toward the car. Shonte Jr. hung back, speaking low-voiced to his brother. He said, "Lee Harvey, I don't get you. Why you helping them find Daddy?"

Whispering back, Lee Harvey said, " 'Cause we gonna need to be there when these lyin-ass flunkies find 'em . . . or who knows what'll happen."

Chapter Nine

Hank was chain-smoking when he started coughing. It began as a tickle in the throat, which he tried to clear several times without success. Something caught down there, he swallowed wrong, something, and he started coughing. The tumult touched something deep in his chest, setting off a violent coughing fit.

Hank spasmed, unable to stop, his face red, eyes tearing, his whole body flexing.

When the coughing finally stopped, so did Hank.

Charlie was back. He said, "Goddammit!"

Beside him sat Irene, warily watchful. Noticing the lit cigarette he held in one hand, he angrily stubbed it out in the car ashtray.

He said, "Would you please ask him to stop this! It's giving me palpitations."

Irene got it. "Oh, God . . . *Charlie*?"

"Disappointed?" Charlie said, voice tinged with

bitterness. Hank and his lawless antics were really starting to get under his skin.

The last thing Charlie remembered was sitting in the diner's booth, getting ticked off about the bug-eyed kid gawking at him.

Where was he now?

He looked around, discovering that he sat behind the wheel of a car, surrounded by water. It was daytime. Which day, he couldn't say, though he would soon learn that it was only an hour or two since he'd last folded himself up inside his head, making way for Hank.

The car was small, cramped, unfamiliar. The window was rolled down and his elbow was resting on top of the car door. The car was parked on a ferry, which was moving across a large flat lake, whose far-wooded shores were purple-blue with dusky shadows. The sky was still blue and full of light.

He felt different, too. A moment passed before he realized that he was breathing properly through his nose. Tilting the rearview mirror to reflect his image, he studied it in the horizontal looking glass.

His nose was back to normal, with a butterfly-shaped white gauge bandage taped over it. He said, "Hey, my nose, it's fixed."

Irene said, "Yeah, Hank insisted we stop at a plastic surgeon. He was trying to do something nice for you."

Charlie's genuine pleasure soured a trifle. "Yeah, yeah, I'll bet. Mr. Nice Guy."

Reaching to readjust the rearview mirror, Charlie noticed something of which he'd been previously unaware. His chin was swollen and oversized, with a big square white square of gauze taped over it.

He gasped. "What the hell is this?"

"Oh," Irene said. "Hank thought you had kind of a weak chin."

Charlie was outraged. "What?! I like my chin. It's my chin." He felt around the chin, gingerly.

Something else occurred to him. "And how the hell did he pay for it?"

From the back of the car, a voice said, "I loaned him the money."

Charlie started. He'd been unaware that anyone beside him and Irene were in the car. Turning around to look over the top of the seat, he saw the albino waiter from the diner comfortably planted in the back seat.

At Ma's eatery, Charlie had checked out before the waiter had arrived at his table, so the youth with the whiter shade of pale was unknown to him.

He said, "What the . . . ? Who are you?"

The waiter said, "It's me—Milky."

Charlie glanced at Irene, who just shrugged. Charlie turned to face the other, saying, "You mind telling me what you're doing here?"

That nudged the waiter a hair out of joint. He said, "What do you mean? You said you were going to do me a Chuck Woolery Love Connection and fix me up with some albino nymph in Rhode Island, remember?"

Charlie had no memory of it. Even with the windows open, he suddenly felt the tiny car closing in on him. He needed some air. He got out of the car and walked around on the deck of the ferry.

He was leaning his elbows on a rail, looking toward shore, at the landing for which the ferry was making. The albino waiter took up a position beside him, and for a moment the two stood there silently, regarding the nearing shore.

Finally the waiter said, "You wanna get rid of me now, don't you?"

Charlie turned, facing him. "No, I don't want to get rid of you. I just . . . Look, kid, here's the deal: I'm a schizophrenic."

The waiter's attitude suggested that that was no problem. "I know, I know. Hank explained the whole thing to me, how you're a big pussy and he has to fight all your fights and eventually you'll just disappear and he'll be the one."

Charlie, feeling insulted, said, "Anyway, Irene's got a lot of people who would love to see her in an unmarked grave. You don't want to hang around us."

"Why not? You, Irene, and Hank are my friends."

Clearly Charlie wasn't getting through to the other. He tried a new tack. "What about your family? Won't they miss you?"

"My family's all . . . they're gone." The waiter

turned, looking back at the shore, eyes misting. Charlie was seized by a sudden wave of sympathy for the guy.

"Oh, jeez," he said. "Well . . . if you're going to be coming with us, I can't very well be calling you Milky. What's your real name?"

The waiter smiled. "Casper. But my friends call me Whitey."

Hank's misadventures had certainly played hell on Charlie, but at least they'd helped to throw police off the trail. The combined federal, state, and local law enforcement task force assigned to apprehend Charlie and Irene had manpower, resources, computerized data banks, patrol cars, boats, planes, and helicopters. What it didn't have was the two fugitives.

· The dragnet had traced Charlie and Irene as far as Ma's Diner, but no farther. The cops hadn't gotten hip yet to the Whitey connection. They flooded the area, blanketing the roads with prowl cars, but they were looking for Gerke's unmarked sedan, not knowing it slept with the minnows at the bottom of the rock quarry pond.

They weren't looking for Whitey's little Yugo, a battered and scrappy minicar that had outlasted the country that made it. Of course, under such circumstances, the worth of the car warranty was doubtful.

But the car had zipped right past police, boarding the lake ferry. Now, while the hunters still combed the Ma's Diner area, the fugitives drove through the backwoods of New York State, making for Vermont.

An eventful and tiring day, and the coming of night, mandated that Charlie, Irene and Whitey seek lodging for the night at a roadside motel. Whitey's freely advanced funds made the stopover a reality.

Irene went into the motel office to register, while Charlie and Whitey waited in the car. She returned, standing beside the car, lowering her head so that it was framed by an unrolled front window.

She said, "They only had two rooms—10 and 11—so you guys have to double up."

And so they did. The room shared by the males had a lone queen-sized bed, no cable TV, a bureau dresser, and a small side table with two chairs.

Inside the night table drawer, instead of a Gideon Bible, there was a card listing the Ten Commandments. And the motel was so cheap, it had only listed five of them.

Irene was settled in in the next room. Charlie and Whitey made ready for the night. The TV was on, with indecipherable talking heads blah-blahing to each other through a snowstorm of static.

Charlie and Whitey lay stretched out atop the queen-sized bed, laying side-by-side, neither of them looking too comfortable with the arrangement. They both lay fully clothed on top of the bedspread, which had not been pulled back.

Charlie lay with arms folded on the pillow, head

resting atop them, looking up at the cracks in the plaster ceiling.

Making conversation, just to break a stretch of prolonged uncomfortable silence, Charlie began, "So . . . Whitey, what happened to your family?"

"I killed 'em."

"Whuh . . . uh, whuh . . . come again."

Whitey was nonchalant, not bragging, his manner that of one who is simply stating the facts. "When I was fifteen, I hacked 'em up with a hammer while they were sleeping. Ma, Dad, my bro, and my sis. She was awake—my sis. Which I regret."

Charlie deadpanned, mainly because that part of his face not covered by bandages was stiff with shock. Keeping his voice level, he said evenly, "Oh, well, we all have, you know, family stuff . . . That's why the holidays are so . . ."

Charlie's voice trailed off, into inaudibility. Whitey's pink eyes were slitted, almost closed as he reminisced. "Anyway, I just got released last month on my twenty-first birthday. I wasn't ready to go, but they said I had to. Fucked-up law, huh?"

Charlie, nervous, sat up in bed. "Mm. Wow. That's a heck of a story."

He swung his feet to the floor, standing up. "Hey, you know what? I think I'm going to go next door and try to make out with what's-her-name."

Whitey said, "Go for it."

Charlie went. Stepping outside, he closed the motel room door behind him. Once it was closed, the shoulder blades he'd been holding tensed, in expectation of a knife stabbing between the two of them, relaxed a bit.

He now stood on a paved walkway fronting a row of rooms. Having just quit Number 10, he went next door, knocking on Number 11.

The door wasn't closed all the way and when he knocked, it opened. "Irene . . . ?" Charlie stuck his head inside. Lights were on in the room, the bed was unmade, and Irene seemed absent.

That was worrisome, in light of the ongoing effort to exterminate her. Charlie went into the room, concerned. He approached the bathroom, where the light was on and the door was open a crack. "Irene, you in there?"

No answer. He peeked into the bathroom.

Empty.

Charlie said, "Shoot."

A noise at the doorway caught Charlie's attention. He turned to see Irene coming in from outside, clutching her shoulder bag, moving in an almost stealthy manner. Charlie stood silent in shadow, and she didn't see him as she came in.

Setting the bag down on the bed, she opened it, hands shaking with excitement. Reaching inside, she pulled out the oversized vibrating dildo.

Glimpsing Charlie, she gasped. "Jesus Christ, Charlie, you almost gave me a heart attack."

He stepped forward, into the light. "Where have you been? I was worried about you."

After a pause, she said brightly, "I went to the car to get my bag."

"Oh. Listen, we have a real problem with Whitey," Charlie began, then he saw the dildo. He asked loudly, incredulously, "What are you doing with that?"

"I, uh, I wanted to get rid of this thing once and for all—you know, so Hank doesn't get any more ideas."

"Uh-huh."

She tossed the dildo into a wastebasket beside the night stand. "There."

The thing was so big that inches of flesh-colored plastic shaft, complete with gnarly snakelike veins plus other appendigial unmentionables, stuck out past the top of the basket's circular rim.

Being tossed somehow flicked on the switch, activating the internal vibrator, which hummed and buzzed like a big fat bumblebee in a field of pollinated flowers.

Charlie returned to the problem at hand. "Well, listen, the kid just confessed to me that he butchered his entire family in their sleep."

Irene said, "*What*?!"

Charlie nodded, earnest, intense. "Yeah. He was a minor when he did it. He just got out."

"Oh. So what's the problem?"

Charlie gave her a look. Irene bent over, reaching

into the wastebasket to switch off the vibrating dildo.

Of course, she could afford to view Whitey's confession with a blandly unruffled attitude. She didn't have to sleep in a bed next to him. Charlie was reluctant to return to his room.

As it turned out, Irene wasn't averse to another person's company, either. Being stalked by hitmen was one of those uniquely personal experiences that tend to sharpen one's appetite for social intercourse with others who are not hired killers themselves.

Charlie and Irene started chatting, breaking the ice. Before long, they both sat on the bed, backs against the headboard, as Charlie laid out some pictures of the family back home that he always carried with him.

They were somewhat weathered from his dunking in the rock quarry, wrinkled, but somewhat legible. Clearer at least than the picture on the TV.

Laying down a photo on the bedspread, Charlie said proudly, "That's me and my whippersnappers."

Irene took a close look at the photo. Charlie was playing it straight, beaming at the camera, but Lee Harvey, Jamal, and Shonte Jr. looked like they were posing for mugshots in a police line-up. Lee Harvey wore a bandana covering his nose and mouth, Jamal wore wraparound hipster sunglasses over a coldly hostile face, and Shonte Jr. glared, making gang-style hand signals.

Unsure how to react, Irene said, simply, "Precious."

Charlie laid out another photo, this one depicting him and the lads dressed as characters from *The Wizard of Oz*.

He said, "Here we are again. I'm Dorothy."

"When was this picture taken, Halloween or something?"

"Nah, we were just messing around at home."

Irene smiled. "You seem like a good dad, Charlie."

"I try to be."

"Uh, if you don't mind me asking, how is it that—?"

"I know," Charlie said, grinning. "How can a guy who looks like me have a lion for a son? It's a long story."

"I believe it," she said.

He said, "They're incredible kids. Funny, happy, they don't give me any grief. They're the top three in their class out of 212 students."

"You're a lucky guy. I don't think I carry even one photo anymore."

"Why not?"

"I don't know, I had some pictures of friends when I was younger, and then they got old and fell apart." She felt a touch of the blues. Sadly, she added, "Just like the friendships, I guess."

She looked away, remembering. Breaking the awkward silence, Charlie put forward one of his photos. He said, "Hey, why don't you take this one." It was *The Wizard of Oz* photo.

Irene shook her head. "No, I can't. It's yours."

"Are you kidding? Take it, I have a bunch at home. Seriously, take it."

She took it, looking at him fondly. There was a silence. Charlie thought seriously about kissing her, but when it came down to it, he lacked the nerve.

Hopping up, he said, "I'm dry. You know what, I'm going to get myself a soda. You want one?"

Outside, a couple of doors away, standing against the wall, was an oversized slab of a soda vending machine, its colorful front glowing with lights and rainbow hues. Charlie stood facing it, feeding quarters to the machine's hungry slot.

He put in the correct amount of change, then pressed the button for Coke. Processes sounded from inside the machine, the *sproing* of a suddenly released spring, the *ka-chung*! of a weighty object dropping into place through the dispensing rails, and a snapping sound as servomotors opened the hinge at the top of the plastic-screened hopper that would receive the soda can.

Everything worked properly, except that nothing dropped into the hopper.

No can of Coke, or any other soda.

Nada.

Charlie checked the Coke button. According to the lighted panel, the machine wasn't out of Coke.

Charlie jiggled the coin return lever a few times, working it. For his efforts, he received no quarters and no Coke.

It was all very irksome. Oily drops of sweat started on Charlie's forehead. His eyes were hot, intent, his face strained.

Reaching into his pants pocket, he fished out some more quarters and repeated the process, feeding them into the slot. He dropped them in carefully, one at a time, making sure that he heard each one *ching*! into place, registering its presence before feeding in the next coin.

When the requisite sum of coins was once more put in, Charlie very carefully and forcefully—but not too forcefully—pressed the Coke button to make his selection.

Same sounds—no Coke.

Charlie stood there, facing the machine, doing a slow burn.

From behind him came a rude chuckle. Slowly Charlie turned, seeing the source of the derisive laughter, another of the motel guests, a man who was unpacking luggage from his car trunk.

The chuckler said, "I saw that. Not once, but twice it got you."

He snickered again, nastily, then slammed his trunk shut.

In the depths of Charlie's black-pupiled eyes, Hank stirred, threatening to swim to the surface.

In Room 11, stretched out on top of the bed, Irene heard some banging noises from outside, but they quickly subsided and she thought no more about them.

A moment later, Charlie—*Charlie*?!—entered the room, smiling cheerfully, holding a can of Coke in each hand.

He announced, "I just had an epiphany!"

Irene said sympathetically, "I have some Maalox in my purse."

Charlie shook his head. "No, I just discovered something about myself."

"What?"

"That I can control this little problem of mine."

Irene stirred, sitting up. "How did you discover that?"

"First the Coke machine robbed me—I can handle that—but then some guy laughed in my face."

"Uh-oh."

"No, that's just it. Just when I was starting to follow that familiar pattern of mine, I decided to take a few deep breaths, count backwards from ten, and laugh right along with him. I even helped him with his luggage."

Irene relaxed, tension leaving her limbs. "That's great. And you got the Cokes, too."

He brandished the Cokes victoriously, holding them aloft in triumph. "A little rap to the side of the machine and presto."

He tossed her a can. "The point is, I'm getting smarter. I'm learning to deal with things."

Irene leaned over the bed's edge, reaching down into her bag and pulling out the half-gallon bottle of rum that Hank had bought earlier.

Smiling sunnily, she said, "Look what I found in my bag. Do you drink?"

Charlie reached to stroke his chin thoughtfully, but the bandages from the plastic surgery chin job got in the way. "Under the right circumstances, yeah, I could tip a few."

Irene stood up, getting a couple of the motel's paper-wrapped clear plastic cups and mixing two rum-and-cokes. "You're a piece of work, you know that?"

He nodded. Irene laughed, said, "What was your dad like?"

Charlie winced with emotional pain, trying and failing to cover it up. Irene realized she had hit a nerve with him.

He said, "Oh, my dad was a great guy. I didn't see a lot of him 'cause he was always out with his friends and stuff—he had a lot of friends. But when he was around, boy, you sure knew it. He was so funny and loud and . . . he could get so loud sometimes . . ."

Charlie looked haunted, undoubtedly reliving traumatic memories of childhood abuse. Gamely, he went on. "But you know, it was a different era and people spanked their kids back then. They hit 'em some good ones sometimes. But . . . I was a colicky baby, too, you know. I must've driven the poor guy crazy."

Somehow, he forced a smile. "He was a good man. Strong as an ox."

There was an awkward moment, broken as Irene handed him his drink. Charlie lifted his plastic cup, finding the inner strength to carry on and seize the moment.

Smiling fragilely, he toasted, "To Dad."

Irene clinked her cup against his, and they drank. The mix was hot in her mouth, rum-heavy, burning a line of fire down her gullet and into her belly, warming it.

Perhaps she'd made the drinks overstrong. Oh well, what was the worst that could happen—a hangover?

Chapter Ten

CHARLIE AWOKE. HE FELT BRAIN-NUMBED, woolly-headed, shaky. He climbed out of bed, standing up, supporting himself by resting a hand on the headboard. All he wore was a pair of boxer undershorts printed with big yellow happy faces.

The lamps were dark, but the room was filled with gray dawn light filtering in through the window curtains. On the night table stood a half empty bottle of rum. In bed, Irene lay curled on her side, facing him, sleeping, the sheets and blankets pulled up over her shoulders. Her hair spilled across the pillow. In the low light, her face was a soft pink oval. She sighed, murmuring, eyelashes fluttering.

Charlie groggily stumbled into the bathroom. Standing over the toilet, he started to pee, but he was surprised when the yellow stream squirted off to the side, in an unexpected direction.

That certainly was a puzzler. He called out, "Irene . . . ?"

After he called her name a number of times, louder each time, she answered, saying drowsily, "Yeah . . ."

"Um, why am I peeing like I was up all night having sex?"

Outside, the dragnet was closing in. The police had finally tracked the fugitives to the motel. Now, the authorities circled the place, surrounding it with a cordon of police cars, a squad of uniformed patrolmen, a SWAT team, and a cadre of federal agents.

In charge of the operation was Agent Boshane, with Lieutenant Gerke sticking close to his side.

The dawn mists were laced with adrenaline and testosterone, as the police squads itched with eagerness to make the raid, big beefy cops trembling with excitement like racehorses in the starting gate, waiting for the bell to be up and at 'em.

Boshane cautioned, "I want everyone to stay put and wait for my orders."

This would be tricky, and must be handled just right. It would be well if neither Charlie nor Irene were taken alive, but were instead shot safely dead "while resisting arrest."

In the motel room, Charlie was resisting facing the truth about last night, but awareness kept oozing in around the edges. The last thing he clearly remembered was standing outside at the soda machine, which was eating his quarters and giving nothing in return. Yes, and there was also some character unloading the luggage from the trunk of his car, giving Charlie the horse laugh because of his difficulties with the soda machine. Beyond that, all was blank.

Pale and angry, Charlie got dressed. Irene stood off to one side, not meeting his gaze. He said, "I would really like to know what went on here last night."

That stung a little hot color into Irene's cheeks. "Don't even joke, Charlie. This isn't funny."

"Yeah, I know it's not. You don't see me laughing." He faked a laugh, sounding as hollow as an empty tomb. "That's laughing. You don't hear that, do you?"

Comprehension came flooding into Irene's awareness. Her eyes widened and her mouth became a round, shocked O. "You mean . . . ? You're telling me that I . . . ?

"Oh, God."

Remembering something from last night, she said, "Charlie, what was your father like?"

"Greatest guy who ever walked the face of this earth. Why?"

Irene sagged, the wind taken from her sails. Her shoulders slumped. Her knees went rubbery, and she sat down hard on the edge of the bed, devastated.

Stunned, she said, "I thought . . . you see . . . when you came back . . . *Hank tricked me*."

Charlie was having none of it. "He tricked you into giving him a hickey on my ass? That's some trick, lady—you've got to teach me that one."

Irene stopped feeling bad and got mad, jumping up. "Hey, fuck you, man! I'm the one who should be pissed. I thought he was you."

"Okay, all right, okay." Charlie backed away, a bit sheepish, but after a few beats his long-simmering resentment at Hank flared up.

He said, "No, it's not okay. It's not okay! All right?! You mean to say you couldn't tell the difference between us?"

Irene stared at him in disbelief. "Are you serious? Who the hell could?"

He indicated the well-tippled rum bottle. "A sober person, for one."

Irene said, "Okay, so we had a drink . . . or two."

It was all too much for Charlie. He had to sit down. Besides, he was hurting. He didn't know if it was the aftereffects of the booze or what, but the inside of his skull felt like an exploded bomb crater, and his ass felt like it had been reamed out by Roto-Rooter.

He sat on the bed, dizzy. He noticed something under the covers. Gingerly, with delicate distaste, using his thumb and forefinger, he fished out the dildo, hauling it into view.

He said, "Ah, look who joined the party. So I guess old Hank wasn't enough for you, huh?"

Irene cleared her throat. "Um . . . it wasn't for me."

At that moment, it all came crashing down on

Charlie. Looking green around the edges, he said, "I don't feel so good."

He'd have felt even worse had he known of the noose of the law inexorably tightening around him and Irene. At that moment, while the police minions circled the motel, staking it out, Agent Boshane was interrogating the motel manager, doing the detail work to ensure that this time there would be no fuck-ups.

Boshane himself was being watched, by Charlie's three sons, who were sticking close to the top cop in charge of the operation. Boshane, Gerke, Lee Harvey, Jamal and Shonte Jr. were all crowded into the manager's office, where the walls were made of caramel-colored varnished pine.

The manager was balding, his high-topped skull gleaming as if it, too, was another piece of woodwork buffed and polished to a high gloss. He stood behind the check-in counter, with Boshane and Gerke standing on the other side, facing him. Lining the wall were the three brothers, listening intently.

The manager said, "I called when I saw the paper."

On the counter was a newspaper folded to display its front-page photos of Charlie and Irene. Tapping a finger against Irene's picture, Boshane said, "Are you positive that's the woman you saw?"

The manager was certain. "Oh, that's her, all right. She caught my attention because she rented two rooms . . . 10 and 11."

Boshane and Gerke exchanged glances. Boshane slid the newspaper across the counter, returning it to the manager. The fed said, "Thanks for your help."

He and Gerke went outside, with the Baileygates brothers trailing. The sky was gray. The early morning was clammy, chilly. The motel's outside lights were still on, burning palely against the fuzzy grayness of predawn gloom.

Boshane and Gerke went to Boshane's command cruiser, parked out of sight behind a corner of the motel. They were faced by Shonte Jr., Lee Harvey and Jamal.

Shonte Jr. said, "Let us go talk to Daddy. This don't have to be no big thing."

Gerke said, "Thanks, fellas, but this is the end of the line for you. Stubie is going to drive you back to the chopper."

Stubie came shambling up, nodding, head bobbing. Jamal's sharp-featured face twisted into a lip curling sneer. "What?! You brung us all the way down here for us to leave now?"

Lee Harvey was resolute, rock-hard. "That don't make no motherfuckin' sense."

Gerke seemed not unsympathetic. "You guys have done all you can do. This is strictly a police matter from here on in."

Jamal said, "It's a police matter to you, but the police don't matter shit to me when it's my daddy in there."

Gerke glared at him. So much for the sympathy

bullshit. Now it was time to lay down the law. "I said you're getting the hell out of here. That's the end of it."

He turned, walking away. Boshane, uncomfortable, turned to the brothers. "I'm sorry, guys. Between you and me, the guy's a dickhead, but in this case he happens to be right. I can't allow you to be here—it's a liability thing."

Lee Harvey pointed at Gerke. "He's the motherfuckin' liability."

Boshane said, with a show of sincerity, "Well, don't worry. I'm going to make sure we resolve this thing without bloodshed."

Stubie drove up in his cruiser. The brothers exchanged looks. Stubie motioned for them to get in. Shonte Jr. opened the passenger side door and flopped down into the front seat, crowding the hefty Stubie. Then Lee Harvey got in, cramming himself into the front seat, too, somehow getting the door shut. It looked like one of those clown cars in the circus, where a mob of clowns get out from a tiny car. This cop cruiser wasn't small, it just looked that way, with all that flesh sandwiched behind the windshield.

Jamal got into the back seat. Stubie rolled the car out of the motel lot, down the road.

In the motel room, behind a closed bathroom door, Charlie tended to himself. He'd been in there for a long time. Irene, concerned, stood outside the closed door.

She said, "Charlie? You okay?"

He stood with his pants and shorts down to his ankles, his bare ass pressed up against the sink, as he splashed his butt cheeks with cool running water from the faucet.

With grim cheer, he called back, "Yep. I'm just freshening up."

Outside, nearby, Boshane and Gerke huddled beside the command cruiser, putting their heads together to hatch out a foolproof execution strategem. Boshane said, "So, how do you want to handle it?"

Gerke said flat-out, "I say we storm the place and start shooting."

"What if he's unarmed?"

"We'll plant a gun on him afterwards," Gerke said, not bothering to hide the contempt in his voice. The fed was something of a softie. No wonder the operation had been a botch so far.

He said, "You heard what Dickie said—he wants them both dead, no excuses."

Boshane stared across the parking lot at the door to Number 11. He didn't much care for Gerke jerking his chain, reminding him that they were both working for Dickie.

The agent said, "Well, don't fuck it up this time."

Boshane reached into the cruiser, pulling out an pump-action riot shotgun. Gerke unholstered his piece, a 9mm Beretta semi-automatic pistol, flat and black.

Boshane motioned, signaling his assault squad to

move in. He would lead the raiders, with Gerke beside him. That was better than having Gerke behind him, with a drawn gun. His association with the bad lieutenant was strictly a matter of convenience—a temporary arrangement.

Led by Boshane and Gerke, the team fell into position, some crouching behind cars, others hustling up beside the building, all of them armed with enough firepower to overthrow a medium-sized country.

Boshane and Gerke led a group of three others towards the doors of Rooms 10 and 11. Boshane pointed the shotgun at the door of Number 11, preparing to blow the lock off the door and crash in. He'd be the first in, Gerke would stand in the doorway blocking the others, giving Boshane enough time to put the blast on Irene and anyone else in the room.

Just then, one of the cops crouched behind a police car stood up, waving his portable radio handset. "Lieutenant!"

The raiders all turned to face each other. The cop with the handset said, "It's Stubie, sir. They've got Baileygates and the girl!"

Gerke showed open-faced astonishment. "What?!"

That took the lead out of their pencils. The squad deflated, lowering their gun barrels. Gerke and Boshane stalked over to the command cruiser. Gerke contacted Stubie via the two-way police radio. "Gerke here. What's going on?"

Stubie said, "We're out on Highway 134." There must have been something wrong with the transmission since Stubie's normally pear-shaped tones sounded thin, strained.

He said, "I caught 'em in a stolen vehicle—Baileygates and the girl. I got 'em!"

Gerke and Boshane were goosed by alarm. This was not good. Boshane grabbed the handset from Gerke, speaking into it. "Stubie, I don't want you to attempt to move them alone, do you hear me? Don't fucking move them! We'll be right there."

Stubie wasn't going anywhere. His cruiser was pulled off to one side of the road, standing under some dew-dripping pines. Stubie himself was dripping, his round smooth face shiny with sweat, his eyes bulging.

Beside him sat Lee Harvey, holding Stubie's own gun trained on the policeman. In the back seat were Jamal and Shonte Jr.

Stubie hung up the handset.

Lee Harvey said, "Like motherfuckin' butter, Officer. You could be a'actor."

The cloud of dust left behind by the police cars as they raced away to rendezvous with Stubie still hung in the air as Charlie and Irene emerged from Number 11, oblivious to their narrow escape. Charlie was disheveled, pale and dejected.

Irene was momentarily distracted by the sight of

a battered and broken soda machine, with a red fire axe buried in its side. Turning her attention to the problem at hand, she said, "What do we do about Whitey?"

Charlie said, "Take a guess. We're going ahead without him."

"Wow. *Moo-dee*."

They spoke low-voiced, mindful of the nearness of the door of Number 10.

Charlie groused, "Well, I'm sorry but I didn't have the fun you had last night. I just got the hangover and the swollen prostate."

Irene rolled her eyes. Charlie said, "How much change do you have from when we checked in?"

Irene said, "Sixty-two bucks, but it's Whitey's."

"Yeah, well, if he hadn't killed his family, we wouldn't have to be ditching him, now would we?"

So, it had come to this. Now he was stealing Whitey's money. Even if it was nicely motivated, it was a helluva comedown for a Rhode Island state trooper.

Must be Hank's influence, Charlie told himself.

With the heavy police presence, it didn't take long for Stubie's cruiser to be found. Now Stubie was freed and Charlie's three sons apprehended. Police vehicles ringed Stubie's car, whose backseat now held Lee Harvey, Jamal, and Shonte Jr., all three in handcuffs.

Gerke roasted Stubie, heaping rhetorical hot coals on his hapless head, finishing up by saying, "I don't believe this shit!"

A gap opened in the knot of cops ringing Stubie's cruisers, giving the irate police lieutenant a glimpse of the Baileygates brothers.

Gerke roared, "Get these dirtbags out of my sight!"

Stubie waddled to his car, sliding behind the wheel and driving away, toward the nearest police station. Boshane, Gerke, and the rest of the cops zoomed back to the motel. But the slice of time that Lee Harvey, Jamal and Shonte Jr. had bought by leaning hard on Stubie had been enough.

When the police returned, Whitey was already up and sitting behind the wheel of his car, reading the note which he'd found where it'd been slipped under the motel room door.

It said:

WHITEY—HAD TO GO. TOO DANGEROUS FOR YOU. BORROWED A FEW BUCKS. WILL PAY BACK. MY ADDRESS IS BELOW. YOUR PALS, CHARLIE AND IRENE.

Below which was written Charlie's address in Jamestown, Rhode Island. His real address, not some made-up one, although Whitey didn't know that yet.

Whitey was unhappy. Snowy eyebrows knitted in a ferocious frown as he read the note, making him look like a white owl, an unhappy white owl. His face was as closed and tight as a fist.

His unhappiness only increased as a handful of police cruisers came screeching into the motel parking lot. He didn't know Boshane and Gerke from Adam, but now he knew the faces of the plainclothes federal agent and the police lieutenant, who were the first to arrive, kicking in the doors of Rooms 10 and 11, barging in with drawn guns, only to emerge empty-handed in paroxysms of new frustration.

If the cops had looked at the other end of the lot, they'd have seen Whitey. But the lawmen were shortsighted.

That's because Boshane and Gerke were calling the shots, and they both had a hidden agenda, one that was driving the imperatives of the manhunt. And womanhunt.

After a while, the cops all got back into their cars and went away. Whitey watched them go. More time passed, then he left, too.

Charlie and Irene were in the area, within walking distance of the motel, at a train station. A lonely site, it featured a Gothic-style brick station house with pointed-arch windows and a sleepy, white-haired old stationmaster dozing off behind the ticket wicket, dreaming of how he'd missed catching the last train to Hooterville, Mayberry, and similar way stations.

Charlie made the call from a pay phone outside the station, on the side facing the tracks. Irene sat on a nearby bench.

Charlie's latest brainstorm was to contact someone he knew he could trust, and who would be able
to handle the situation professionally. That meant the
fellows from his state trooper barracks, specifically
Captain Partington.

Charlie called the captain's office number. The
phone rang for a long time before it was picked up.
Maryann was at the other end of the line. Attempting
to disguise his voice, Charlie asked for Captain Partington. She said he was unavailable. Charlie didn't
want to identify himself, so he said he'd call back
later and hung up. Another idea came to him. He
called one of his fellow troopers, someone he could
trust.

The other was at home, picking up when Charlie
called. "Finneran, it's me, Charlie."

Squawking sounded from the other end, but Charlie cut it off, in a hurry. He said, "Never mind that,
that's why I called you at home. I need you to get
a message to the captain."

Finneran got the message, holding a phone
pressed to his ear by one shoulder while he jotted
down the information on a notepad.

Reading it back to confirm, he said, "Four-thirty
at the South County train station, and bring plenty
of backup. You got it."

Finneran reassured Charlie, "No, I won't tell anyone outside the department."

Charlie thanked him a million.

Finneran said, "Yeah. See you then."

The connection was broken. Finneran opened his billfold, taking out a slip of paper on which was written a mobile phone number. He dialed it.

"This is Finneran here. You were right. He called."

At the other end of the line, Agent Boshane said, "Four-thirty, huh? Well, thanks for notifying us, Officer. That's a big help."

Boshane hung up his cell phone. His neck was on the line and it was time to begin sharing out some of the pain. He said, "Where's Dickie?"

Gerke said offhandedly, "Waiting for us in New York."

"Well, I think it's time the little rich boy got his hands dirty."

Chapter Eleven

CHARLIE AND IRENE SAT ON A BENCH, FACING THE railroad tracks, waiting for a train. Charlie was deeply disturbed by the swathe Hank had been cutting through his life. Unsettling to be your own love rival!

He was spoiling for a fight, and since Hank wasn't around, Irene would have to do. He said, "So, come on, let's hear it. How was Mr. Wonderful?"

Irene, confused, said, "*How was he?*"

"You know."

She saw where he was going, and it irked her. She said, "It's none of your damn business."

"I beg to differ, but I think it is my business when it's my liver that's getting pickled in the process."

Irene nervously ran her fingers through her hair. Adding to her discomfort was the awful truth that Charlie was, indeed, a mental case—literally. She didn't want him to get worked up and excited, for fear of what—or who—might emerge.

She said, "This is fucked up, Charlie. Just let it go."

No way he was going to let it go, not when he was working up a nice full load of righteous indignation. "Yeah, it's fucked up all right. I turn my back and what do you do? You stick it up my ass! Literally."

Headjob or not, Charlie dumped on Irene enough. Now she was good and mad. "Yeah, and it slid in there pretty damn easy, too."

Charlie squirmed in his seat, abashed. "So, I've had a couple of sigmoidoscopies."

"What did they use—the periscope from a submarine?"

That threw him momentarily. Shaking his head, he tsk-tsked. "Boy oh boy. In this day and age, to be jumping in the sack with a guy you just met. You have no idea what you could catch from a creep like that."

"Look, Charlie, now *I'm* starting to feel sick. I got news for you—it takes three to tango."

Charlie made a face, snippily shaking his head. "Oh, I think you and Hank did the tangoing—I'm just the one who got blisters on my feet, remember?"

"How can I forget? You haven't stopped whining about it since you woke up!"

"Hey, don't turn this around on me. You're the one who can't keep your legs closed."

Irene ran out of energy for argument. She fell silent, turning away from him on the bench, turning

her back to him. Her slim shoulders shook with sti-
fled sobbing. Her dewy eyes squeezed out tears.

Whatever Charlie had wanted, this wasn't it. He
was at a loss for words, not knowing what to say.

Still showing her back, Irene said, "Why are you
doing this?"

Charlie reached for her from behind, to put a com-
forting touch on her shoulder, but he held back, hand
extended, hesitating.

He blurted, "I'm doing it because . . . because I
love you!" Catching himself, he quickly amended,
"Like you."

Irene turned, her face wet with tears. "You . . .
you what?"

Charlie, embarrassed, started to tighten up. "I . . ."

"Yeah?"

"Like you. I'm not afraid to admit it. I, I like you,
Irene. I do."

Irene softened. "Well, you shouldn't. I'm a ditz,
Charlie. Always have been."

He was amazed, flabbergasted. "A ditz? What are
you talking about? You're twenty-seven years old
and you were superintendent of a major golf resort."

She stopped meeting his eyes, looking away guilt-
ily. "I kind of fudged my resume to get that."

"Oh?"

"The truth is, I didn't know the first thing about
running a gold course. I was a model."

"Huh?"

"I moved to New York, but it didn't work out so

I tried to be an actress but I got this eating disorder where I gained twenty pounds."

"That's not so much."

"In a week," Irene said. It all came out in a rush. "Anyway, long story short, none of it worked out and pretty soon I had seventy-year-old guys wanting to support me but I didn't like who I was becoming so I had my breast implants removed and got the job at the golf course, but I ended up sleeping with my boss." She sighed. "I made some big mistakes, Charlie."

That was a lot for Charlie to swallow, but somehow he managed. Now for the big question:

"But, Irene, you didn't know what Dickie was up to, right?"

Brushing away tears with the back of her hand, she looked up. "I'm a ditz, Charlie, but I'm not a crook."

After all that, what else was there to do but kiss her?

So he did.

Whitey was in a less amicable mood, perhaps, as he pulled up in the dirt parking lot of a roadside gun dealer's shop. The albino youth went inside, where just beyond the front door he was greeted by a larger-than-life image of Charlton Heston, superstar actor and straight-shooting NRA prexy.

It wasn't really him, of course, it was a cardboard cutout photodisplay. The Grizzly Adams lookalike behind the other side of the glass gun display counter was real, though. He was big and burly, with a holstered pistol worn high on his hip.

Whitey said, "I need a gun and a lot of ammo."

The gun dealer shook his shaggy head. "Sorry. Seventy-two-hour wait—federal law."

Whitey did some quick calculation, red eyes squinting. "How far am I from Rhode Island?"

The owner shrugged. "Four or five hours. I've got a map of New England if you want—dollar ninety-five."

Whitey was in a hurry to do something. He threw down a five-dollar bill, grabbed the map, and rushed for the exit door. Over his shoulder, he said, "Keep the change."

The owner, grinning, called out, "That's mighty white of you!"

The Baileygates brothers were in the slammer, locked up behind bars in the same holding cell, in a smalltown Vermont jail so cornball that at any minute, they expected to see a New England version of Deputy Barney Fife come running in, all in a tizzy because some fresh kids had sassed Aunt Bea.

In the cell, Lee Harvey, Jamal, and Shonte Jr. slumped around glumly, downcast. On the other side of the bars sat Officer Stubie, who'd been left behind by Lieutenant Gerke to guard the prisoners while the rest of the team continued the pursuit of the fugitives. Stubie had made himself right at home, setting up a portable chess set on a table and working out a chess problem against himself, while he snacked on a sack of fast-food, cheeseburgers, fries, and a megasize vanilla milkshake made from the finest powdered chalk.

He was sharing the watch with one of the two or three local cops that were assigned to the station in this tiny Vermont town.

Now that Stubie was settled in with his chow, it was the Vermont cop's turn to get something to eat. The cop rose from his chair, coming out from behind his desk.

He said, "I'll be back in twenty."

Stubie said, "You bet."

The local lawman went out, leaving Stubie alone in the jail with the prisoners. Stubie took a big bite out of a cheeseburger, meat juices dripping down his chin, making it shiny. He moved a piece on the chessboard, turning the board so he could counter the ploy from the other side.

Lee Harvey said, "What you doing moving that queen's rook? You trying to lose?"

Stubie was still plenty sore about the trick the lads had played him earlier that day, namely taking his gun and putting him under it, forcing him to make the fake radio call that enabled Charlie and Irene to escape.

He demanded, "What're you talking about?"

"You left the king's ass wide open."

"I'll let you know when I need your advice," Stubie said, going back to the chessboard. He started to move his piece, but when he did, he saw that it opened him to a whole other line of attack. Sure enough, Lee Harvey had been right.

Now Jamal took up his part, chiming in. "Lee Harvey, give the man some slack. He's obviously new to the game."

Stubie snorted, waving a dismissive hand. "New? I don't think so. I'm the best chess player back at my precinct."

Lee Harvey said, "Oooh."

"Hey, it ain't bragging if it's true."

"What are you talking about? That's exactly what bragging is. If it weren't true, it'd be lying."

Stubie frowned, thinking that one over. His small, shiny dark eyes glittered from way back in rolls of fat, like a pair of holes poked in a pasty white doughball.

Jamal said, "Hey, Boris Spastic, why don't you play my man, Shonte Jr., here? He got game."

Stubie, moderately interested, tried to hide it. "I'm in the middle of this one."

"Tell you what: You take whatever side's ahead and he'll take the other. Oh, and I'll put ten bucks on him."

Stubie laughed at the absurdity of it, greed winning out. "All right, you're on. I'll take black."

He pushed the small table to the bars of the cell, keeping it between him and the three prisoners, carefully staying out of reach of any desperate getaway attempts. Chuckling at his own cleverness set his many chins rolling. The folding chair creaked dangerously, straining under his weight as he sat down at the table.

Shonte Jr. moved to the bars, within reach of the chess pieces. "Whose turn?"

Stubie said, "Yours."

Shonte Jr. scanned the board, making a quick move. "Checkmate."

Oh, Stubie blustered and squealed, but when he finally quieted down and eyed the board, his face fell with the realization that he'd been instantly, utterly defeated.

Jamal said, "Pay up."

Somewhere in the office, a phone rang. Grunting, then groaning, Stubie rose from his chair. "Don't move. We're playing again."

Shonte Jr. said easily, "I ain't going nowhere."

Stubie walked to the other side, answering the phone. It was a routine call, some old bat calling to complain that her neighbor's kids were making too much noise and she wanted it stopped, pronto!

While Stubie held the phone pressed to his ear, he turned his back on the holding cell. Lee Harvey stealthily reached his hand through the bars, picking up the salt shaker. He unscrewed the cap, dumping the whole bottle of salt on the juicily absorbent burger, covering up the whole mess with the top bun. He put everything back the way he'd found it; all in all, the work of no more than sixty seconds.

Jamal, low-voiced, said, "What the fuck you trying to do, piss him off?"

Lee Harvey said, "You never heard of hypernatremia?"

Jamal gave him one of those don't-mess-with-me-sucker looks. " 'Course I did. Excessive sodium in the blood—what about it?"

"Well, that's gonna make hisself disoriented. Maybe he'll fuck up, give us an opening."

Shonte Jr. said, "Let me get this straight. You trying to salt your way out of prison? That's fucking lame."

Lee Harvey fired back, "Well, what you got?"

Stubie managed finally to get off the phone. Hanging up, he waddled back to his seat at the chess table, his masses of fat jiggling and quaking. The chair lost a couple of inches of height when he sat down on it.

He grabbed the burger and dug in, working on it like a human shredding machine, gobbling it down, chowing down big-time. He must've noticed the excessive salt, at least subliminally, because he washed the burger down by chugging the vanilla milkshake. Having fed the inner man, he returned to the game board.

An hour later, Stubie was well on the road to physical and mental incapacitation. His hand, limp as a dead fish, tried to move a bishop but failed, dropping it.

He was in a stricken state, eyes dulled, jowls

drooping, a thin shiny line of spittle dribbling down from a corner of his slack, downturned mouth.

Speech slurred, he droned, "Ith it thtill my turn?"

The Baileygates brothers put their heads together. Jamal said, "Holy shit. You gave the cat a motherfuckin' stroke."

Lee Harvey said, "I told you it would work!"

Jamal stroked his chin, thinking. "I got an idea."

Stubie, half-conscious, sat uneasily, weaving, swaying, trying vainly to focus on the game. Jamal said suddenly, sharply, "Hey, Officer, what you waiting for? Open the door!"

Stubie stirred slightly from his glaze-eyed torpor, staring blearily at the speaker. "Huh?"

"Do what Lieutenant Gerke said and let us out of here."

That name evoked a response in Stubie's numbed brain, causing a spasm of fear to swim up on his shiny, rosy-red, puffy face. "Lieutenant Gerke? When did. . . . When did he . . . ?"

Jamal kept up the pressure. "He came down here not five minutes ago and told you to set us free! Where the hell's your head at, man?"

Stubie just stared at them.

Lee Harvey said, "*Hello!*"

Stubie started. "Huh . . . ? Oh yeah. I'm thorry, I'm a little . . . out of thorts today."

He opened the jail door, letting the guys out. They wasted no time making an exit. The holding cell cot looked inviting, so Stubie stretched out on it. He was awfully tired. He'd just take a little rest.

The Baileygates brothers went outside. The police station sat on a wide open field. There was little cover, nowhere to hide.

But the open flatness had its advantages, too, since it had served as a landing pad for the New York State Police helicopter that had flown Boshane and Gerke to this area to continue after the fugitives.

The lads all froze at the sight of the whirlybird, sitting there parked on the lawn behind the station, alone and unguarded.

They climbed into the Plexiglas bubble cockpit, Jamal hopping into the pilot's seat. Before him lay a complex instrument panel, which he studied for a minute.

Then he started pushing buttons and throwing switches. Contact was made, the engine was started, the rotor blades starting to turn slowly, accompanied by the rising hum of power as the motor came to life.

The blades spun, whirling, the copter shaking. Jamal's two brothers looked alarmed. Shonte Jr. said, "You know how to drive one of these birds?"

Jamal said, "No. But the console's pretty self-explanatory and I understand the physics of it. It's just about lift, drag, and rotation."

Lee Harvey said, "Well, then get this motherfucker in the air!"

Jamal threw more switches, working the control stick. He must have done something right, for the helicopter lifted up into the air, making eggbeater noises as it whoof-whoofed away.

Chapter Twelve

CHARLIE AND IRENE BOARDED THE TRAIN, GOING to the private compartment for which they'd bought tickets earlier at the station. Since they were hunted fugitives, the compartment would give them much-needed privacy, shielding them from the prying eyes of other passengers who might recognize them from the media coverage and raise the alarm.

The compartment wasn't cheap, but they figured it was worth it. Besides, it was Whitey's money.

Once the conductor had punched their tickets, and they closed and locked the door of the compartment, Charlie and Irene began to relax, a process hastened by their discovery that this was a sleeping compartment, and therefore equipped with bunk beds.

The train plowed through the fields and woodlands and small towns of the Vermont countryside. In the compartment, one thing led to another, and before too long, Charlie and Irene were occupying one bunk bed in the double horizontal position, naked.

Later, a bare-chested Charlie was lying contentedly in his bunk, with Irene snuggling against him. She murmured, "Wow."

Charlie said, "Exactly what I was thinking."

She smiled, then kissed him.

Kisses were far from the mind of Dickie Thurman, who at that very moment was aboard the train, having gotten on at its most recent stop. Boshane had dragged him into the game, making it clear earlier when he'd called Dickie on the cell phone, that they all of them would be in the shitter if Irene and Charlie got away, and that Dickie now must take a more active part in the hunt. No more could he sit back, while Boshane and Gerke were out there in the field, sticking their necks out.

Boshane had the information that too-helpful Finneran had passed along to him, identifying the train the fugitives were taking to Rhode Island. If Dickie moved fast, he could get aboard that train and take care of business well before it reached its destination.

Dickie didn't need much pressure to get his ass in gear. He knew what would happen to him if government prosecutors had Irene testify as a corroborating witness. Clink. That's what'd happen to him. He'd be locked away in the clink for a long, long time. Assuming that they couldn't tie him to having ordered Agent Peterson's murder, in which case he'd be facing the fatal needle, death by lethal injection.

He could be pretty lethal himself, when circumstances demanded it, and they were crying out for it now. He made his way through the train, starting at the lead car, going from car through car toward the end of the train.

The coach cars were an open book, with nowhere to hide, so he breezed through them quite quickly. It was the private sleeping cars that drew his attention, and once he was among them, he moved very, very carefully.

Going from door to door, he'd stop at each, listening in until he'd assured himself that his quarry was not in one, before moving on to the next. Down the long corridor he went skulking, swayed by the rocking train.

All unawares, Charlie and Irene were still cuddled up in the bunk bed, with Irene slowly stroking his bare chest. He looked up at the ceiling, thinking.

"Can I ask you a personal question, Irene?"

"Shoot."

"Did you say 'wow' after you . . . you know, slept with Hank?"

Irene's slow lazy smile of pleasure abruptly turned down at the corners. It was happening again. She began, "Uh, well, I really don't think that—"

"Come on, the truth. It's fine if you did." He

smiled warmly, tolerant, good-hearted, encouraging her.

"Yes, I did," Irene said. "But it was . . . it was a different kind of wow."

Charlie kept worrying at it, not letting it drop. "Stop beating around the bush, Irene. Just tell me the truth: who was better?"

"It's a difficult question to answer, Charlie. I mean, you were both so . . . good in your own way. And different."

"You mean different styles, or he said all the right things, or what? What the hell was so different?"

Irene sighed. "He was bigger."

Charlie didn't know how to handle that one. Abruptly he climbed out of the bunk bed, padding barefoot into the attached bathroom.

Irene lay alone on the bunk, curled on her side, anxiously chewing the tip of a strand of her hair.

Suddenly, the compartment door crashed open, kicked open from outside in the corridor, where Dickie stood, framed in the doorway, gun in hand.

He barged in, closing the door behind him. The lock was broken and wouldn't hold, so he leaned his back against it, keeping it closed. He didn't want any outside interference now, of all times.

Irene, startled, pulled up the covers. Dickie said, "Don't make a sound!"

"Dickie! I—I don't know anything and that's what I told them, I swear."

"Shut up! Just listen to me and maybe we can—"

Something rushed at him from one side, slamming into him, knocking him off-balance. He stumbled forward, tripping, falling, his gun flying from his hand, breaking the window.

He looked up, seeing that what had knocked him down was the bathroom door, opening outward, now revealing Charlie standing in the bathroom with a towel around his waist.

Dickie scrambled to his feet, rushing head-down at Charlie, like a football tackle, slamming him solidly in the middle, knocking the wind out of Charlie as he knocked him back.

Charlie went down, stretching on the bathroom floor, with his bare feet sticking out of the open doorway. Dickie crouched over him, giving him a major-league beatdown, clubbing him with meaty fists.

Irene looked around frantically for something she could use as a weapon. In her bag she found the dildo, which she'd brought along with her after all, for reasons unsure even to herself.

Now, though, it came in handy as she seized it, using it as a club, beating Dickie on the back of the head with it. The set of batteries stored inside it, to power the built-in vibrator, gave it a nice heft.

Dickie slumped to the floor, unconscious. The man pinned beneath him shoved Dickie aside, climbing out from under him and standing up, facing Irene.

Hank said, "Thanks for jumping in. The last thing I need is a manslaughter charge."

Irene groaned, putting a hand to her head. "Oh no, it's you again."

Hank nudged Dickie with a playful kick in the ribs. "What tree did this sap ooze out of?"

Irene said, "It's Dickie—the guy who got me in all this trouble."

Hank's eyes lit up, and he took another look at the face on the bathroom floor. "You mean your golf buddy? Hope he doesn't mind if I play through."

Red color flushed Irene's face. "Hank, knock it off."

"Okay, turn over. I'll play the back nine."

"Stop it!"

Hank lifted an eyebrow, whipping it up like a McDonald's arch. "Come on, this guy couldn't have chewed up the greens that bad."

Irene put her hands on her hips. "This guy hasn't played the course in a while. It was Charlie who was putting."

That came as a surprise, knocking some of the cockiness out of Hank, whose smirk slipped. "Charlie?"

Irene said, "That's right, he may not be long off the tee but he's got a good up-and-down game."

"What the hell's that supposed to mean? Can we talk English for a second?"

Irene reached for the blanket, wrapping it around her, covering up. "Hey, don't give me that shit! I didn't even want to sleep with you—you tricked me!"

"Yeah. I felt bad about that. You know . . . after I came."

Irene said feelingly, "You're an asshole."

Hank pooh-poohed it. "Come on, pussy lips, lighten up."

Irene kicked Hank in the balls, causing him to jackknife in breathless pain. She said, "I warned you about that."

Charlie looked up at her, his face lead-colored, gurgling. "Ughhh. Warned me about what?"

Irene gasped, raising a hand to her open mouth. "Oh, God . . . Charlie. I'm—I'm so sorry. It's just that Hank insulted me."

Charlie grabbed hold of a corner of the bunk bed, hauling himself creakily to his feet. When he stood up, he noticed Dickie, the discovery giving him a violent start. He cried, "Who's that guy?"

Irene sighed. "It's Dickie Thurman."

Charlie's head spun. "Huh? Did you . . . ? What the hell's going on here?"

"I don't know anymore," Irene said. "Look, I'm confused, Charlie. I mean, I know you're a sweet guy and Hank's an asshole, but maybe right now, being in this situation, maybe I need an asshole . . . You know?"

Charlie, in denial, could barely bring himself to say, "You mean you want Hank back?"

Unable to meet his gaze, her head lowered, Irene nodded meekly.

Pain turned to anger, as Charlie declared, "That's it. I've had it with this guy."

Charlie stepped in front of the mirror, facing his reflected image, shaking his fists at it. "Come on out, Hank. Let's settle this thing the old-fashioned way. I may not be tough, but, darn it, I can get good and mad."

It was all too freaky for Irene, especially with Dickie sprawled on the bathroom floor beneath Charlie's bare feet. She said, "Stop it, Charlie, you're scaring me."

The compartment shuddered, shaking and bucking as the train came to a stop.

Over a public address system, a conductor announced, "Pulling into Providence, Rhode Island, in ten minutes. Next stop, South County."

Irene tugged at Charlie's arm, trying to pull him out of the bathroom. She said, "Let's get off before Dickie wakes up."

Charlie wasn't ready to let it go, not yet. Scowling at the mirror, he said, "I'm not finished with you, buster!"

He pulled on some clothes and then he stripped Dickie to his underwear, using the other's belt and necktie to truss up the unconscious man. He threw Dickie's clothes out the window, had an afterthought, went into the bathroom, took off Dickie's shoes, and threw them out the window, too.

He said, "That'll slow him down, if he wakes up. I guess Hank's not the only one around here with ideas!"

He and Irene hurriedly exited the compartment, leaving Dickie still stretched out cold on the bathroom floor.

They went down the corridor to the end of the car, climbing down to the platform of the Providence, Rhode Island, train station. It was a vast, hangarlike structure with parallel lines of tracks that held trains picking up and disgorging groups of passengers. For the fugtives, there was comfort in numbers, with the crowds providing cover to keep them from being spotted by the cops.

But one place where a fellow doesn't want a crowd is inside his head, and as far as Charlie was concerned, two personalities sharing his skull were one too many.

Charlie still couldn't let it go. He muttered, talking to himself—literally. "What's the matter, Hank? Afraid to pick on someone your own size?"

The trouble was, Hank felt the same way about Charlie as Charlie felt about him. Hank caused Charlie to get tripped up by his own feet, destabilizing Charlie so he took a nasty headfirst fall, spilling to the platform pavement.

Passersby stopped to see what had happened. Charlie picked himself up, madder than ever. He said, "Oh, that was dirty—"

Taking on a life of its own, his left hand suddenly grabbed Charlie by the neck, pinning him back against the side of the train and strangling him.

"Hank, you're choking me . . . !"

Charlie's right hand grabbed the wrist of his left hand, trying to break its stranglehold on his neck. The fingers of his left hand were iron bands, sinking deep into his throat, cutting off his air supply.

Charlie's face purpled, bloodshot eyes bulging. Changing tactics, he grabbed one of the fingers on the throttling hand and painfully bent it back, breaking the chokehold.

Hank's persona flashed to the fore, taking possession of the body, pleading. "Ow, ow, ow, ow. No, Charlie, don't break it, don't break it."

Charlie flashed back into place, still bending back that finger, doing damage. "Oh, big tough Hank isn't so scary now, is he?"

Hank returned. "You're right. I'm just a big noise. I'll never chafe you again. I swear, I swear."

"Get on your knees and beg me! Beg me!"

Hank dropped to his knees, pleading. "Please, Uncle Charlie, please don't hurt me."

Charlie's personality crisis had finally blossomed into a full-blown war. Every well-balanced psyche has conflicts with itself, a fact long known to psychiatrists. But Charlie's psyche was imbalanced to the max.

The host body was about to test the truth of Honest Abe Lincoln's assertion that a house divided against itself cannot stand. In this case, the house was Charlie's body. Charlie's mental disruption had grown so great that now he and Hank kept switching back and forth, changing personas in an eyeblink, switching control of the man's body like a channel surfer compulsively switching between two competing programs.

Charlie and Hank warred for control, with the host body as the battlefield. All in all, it was quite the grotesque spectacle, especially for the ever-gathering knot of spectators that stood watching the shenanigans in amazement.

Irene intervened, trying to break it up. "Charlie, let him go!"

Charlie released his grip on his left hand, then stared at Irene. "Oh, you're rooting for him now?"

Now that Charlie was distracted, Hank made use of the diversion to hang one on him. Hank slapped Charlie hard across the face, then karate chopped him across the throat. Charlie fell to his knees, red-faced, sucking air, trying to breathe.

Hank applied the follow-through, reaching around behind himself with the left hand, fingers creeping inside the back of Charlie's waistband to take hold of the top of his undershorts and cruelly yank them up, giving Charlie a brutal wedgie.

The twisted underpants cut painfully against Charlie's soft parts, forcing him to rise to his feet to ease the pulling pain.

Hank grinned savagely, hauling the back of Charlie's undershorts out of the top of his pants. "Get up! I'm not through with you."

The superwedgie turned atomic, ripping the undershorts clear off Charlie's loins, up and out through the top of the back of his pants, a move which left him dazed and confused.

Now Hank had the all-important momentum, the Big Mo. He grabbed Charlie by the hair, getting a big fistful of hair by the roots and tugging it backward. Charlie strained, head tilting back, bandaged chin jutting up, neck cording from the pulling pressure.

Hank most definitely had the upper hand now, and he wouldn't have been Hank if he hadn't taken it to the max. Yanking on the hair, Hank marched Charlie toward a group of blue-haired old ladies who'd come into the big town to do some shopping.

Charlie tried to fight it, but Hank was in control. Charlie's movements were stiff, jerky, like a windup toy soldier with a broomstick up his ass.

Hank said, "Hey, ladies, my name is Charlie Baileygates. I'm a state trooper from Rhode Island. Want to see my weasel?"

Hank pulled down Charlie's pants, exposing himself—themselves—to the goggling golden girls.

Charlie resurfaced long enough to babble, "No, no, no. Don't listen to him. It's Hank, it's Hank!"

The old ladies shrieked and ran—though not before taking a second look.

Hank said, "Zip it!"

He moved quickly to suppress Charlie's pathetic attempts at autonomy, using a cunning move to flip Charlie over on his back, pancaking him to the pavement, stunning him.

It was so stunning, in fact, that Hank backed off, letting Charlie repossess their body so he could feel the big pain of the whomping he'd just given him.

Charlie lay flat on his back, groaning, his limbs thrashing feebly. Then he came to, ready to continue the brawl.

He said to Hank, "Get back here, you pussy!"

Hank was game for more. Charlie jumped to his feet and started beating up himself, battling his way through an exit door, staggering outside into the street.

The party really got rough, as one of the two personalities (even they were unsure by now of who was doing what to whom) tackled the other.

The result was that Charlie crashed backward into a storefront display window, shattering it, tumbling into the place in a shower of broken glass.

Inside the store, people screamed and scattered, fleeing the disintegrating display window and the body tumbling through it, landing with a furious crash on the floor.

Some of the startled onlookers cautiously peeked outside, looking for the assailant who'd just thrown the poor man through the window, only not finding one. Quite a puzzler.

Assailant and victim were both embodied in the

form of one man, who stirred dazedly, shards of broken glass crunching under him as he thrashed weakly on the floor on his his back.

Charlie went limp, exhausted.

Hank shouted, "AUUGGHHH!"

That cry of pain was sweet music to Charlie's ears. He demanded, "Had enough?"

Hank said, "Fuck you!"

Hank spit straight up in the air, the glob falling back down and landing with a splat on Charlie's upturned face.

Charlie said seriously, "That's it. You're dead now."

He rose to his feet, glass shards raining down from him to the floor. Circling himself, looking for an opening, he suddenly feinted, faking himself out, while grabbing hold of himself and hurling himself back out through the shattered window, thudding to the sidewalk, and rolling around in a furious one-man free-for-all brawl.

His self-punishing perambulations cleared the immediate area of spectators, more and more of whom ringed the sidewalk battleground to watch the show.

Irene stood at the edges of the crowd, trying to break through, stymied by the wall of tight-packed gawkers, few of whom were minded to make way. She rose on tiptoes, craning, trying to see what Charlie was doing to Hank, and vice-versa.

An unmarked police car rolled by. In it were Boshane and Gerke, racing to intercept the fugitives when they got off the train. Seeing the commotion outside, the car slowed, creeping past.

The two rogue lawmen couldn't see through the ring of spectators, but one of them spotted Irene at its edges. Immediately the driver hit the brakes, tires screeching. Irene turned, seeing Gerke and Boshane. Their rubber-burning halt distracted the crowd, many of whom turned to eye this latest diversion. Irene used the opportunity to bull her way through the mass of people, slipping sideways between them where possible, and making judicious use of her knees and elbows to make those openings where there weren't any.

Shoving through the last ranks, she saw Charlie rolling around on the sidewalk, trading punches with Hank. Putting her hands on either side of her mouth, megaphone-style, she shouted down at the combatants, "Break it up, you two! It's Gerke!"

Shouts of outrage and cries of pain now sounded, not from Charlie/Hank, but from the spectators, who were being shoved aside by Gerke and Boshane as they tried to break through to the fugitives.

Irene saw an upraised gun in Gerke's hand and took off running, dashing back inside the train station.

Charlie stopped rolling around on the sidewalk. Exhausted, out of breath, he panted, "Okay, truce!"

With his usual good grace, Hank conceded, "Yeah, for now, fucker."

Putting their heads together, they hauled Charlie's

battered body back up to its feet, no easy task considering the punishment they had inflicted on each other.

Charlie started after Irene, who had disappeared through the train station's front entrance. When he dashed clear of the crowd, into the open, Boshane glimpsed him and fired a shot at him. It missed, ricocheting off a stone wall.

The crowd scattered, running for cover, some members shouting and screaming in fear. Boshane swung the gun barrel around, trying to line up another shot at Charlie. Unable to follow Irene into the station without presenting a prime target for the agent's gun, Charlie turned, ducking into an alley.

Gerke ran up, gun drawn. Boshane pointed to the alley, saying, "He went in there! I'll follow the girl, you get Baileygates!"

"Okay!" Gerke went into the alley.

Boshane rushed into the station, holstering his gun. Every second counted and he didn't want to have to waste time flashing his badge to some eager-beager Providence cop. Standing at the head of the tracks, he went from train to train, peering between them in search of Irene.

Irene had just managed to return to the train on which she'd arrived in Providence, mounting a railroad car's steps just as the train lurched forward, pulling out of the station.

Safely on the steps, one hand gripping the rail,

she looked back, searching for some sign of Charlie, but he was nowhere to be seen.

What she did see was Boshane, at the far end of the platform. She ducked back out of sight.

That one glimpse was enough for Boshane, who'd also seen her. He ran after the train, which was picking up speed as it lumbered out of the station. Shoe leather pounding platform pavement, Boshane raced after it, face red, sucking wind, putting on a final burst of speed to overtake the train enough to catch the handrail of the last car, swinging himself up.

Outside the station, the alley down which Charlie had ducked opened at its far end onto a parking lot, where Charlie now crouched behind some parked cars, trying to work out his next move.

Coming up with a bright idea, Hank said, "I'll take the train, you take the alley!"

He ran toward the train. After a half-dozen or so paces he flipped, yielding to Charlie, who immediately turned back, running toward the alley. Hank switched on, heading back for the train, only to be supplanted by Charlie, closing once more on the alley.

Finally he stopped somewhere in the middle, exhausted.

He slumped against a red Mustang, a convertible parked with the top down. What Charlie failed to notice, Hank immediately picked up. Hank whispered, "Take the Mustang—the keys are in the ignition."

Just then, Gerke emerged from the alley, saw Charlie and fired. It was a long shot, clear across the parking lot. The slug tagged Charlie in the arm, knocking him down.

He said, "Oh God, I'm hit."

Hank came to the fore, checking out the injury. Scornfully he said, "It's just a flesh wound, you pussy. Keep moving."

"But I feel . . . I feel faint," Charlie said. Eyes rolling up in the back of his head, Charlie passed out.

This was one time that two heads were better than one. While Charlie was in downtime, Hank took care of business. He said, "Oh, great. You mean to say I've got to carry your ass?"

No reply from Charlie.

Hank hauled himself, and Charlie, too, to their feet. As Charlie, he flopped into the Mustang's passenger seat, slumping unconscious.

Instantly he flipped to Hank, who popped up out of the bucket seat, throwing himself in the driver's seat. He switched on the ignition, firing up the motor.

He said, "We're gone."

He tromped the gas pedal, engine whirring up into high rpms, the car shaking with vibration. The wheels spun, buzzsawing, laying down rubber.

The Mustang jumped off the mark with a screech, peeling out, Hank manhandling the steering wheel, whipping it around to one side, the Mustang slewing around the end of a row of parked cars, turning into a long open lane leading to the street.

Between the Mustang and escape stood Gerke, gun in hand. Seeing the Mustang charging forward, he whirled, swinging his gun toward Charlie.

Charlie said, "Oh, shit . . ."

Hank shouted, "Don't worry about him!"

"But—"

Gerke fired at him, the bullet whizzing past the top of Charlie's head in the open convertible, coming so close that it lifted some strands of his hair.

Hank laughed maniacally. Charlie's foot stepped on the gas, slamming the pedal to the metal, but it was Hank who was in control. The Mustang speeded up, closing on a collision course toward Gerke.

Gerke tried to dodge, but too late. There was a thump as the front of the accelerating car clipped him, knocking him up off his feet. He flew up into the air and over the top of the Mustang before splatting in a very messy pile on the asphalt.

Charlie choked back a sob. Hank snarled, "Can the waterworks, or I'll throw your ass out of the car!"

The Mustang hurtled down the lane, laying rubber. Hank glanced in the rearview mirror, enjoying a last look at the mound of mashed Gerke before cutting into traffic, setting off a frantic tumult of honking horns and screeching tires as other cars had to react swiftly to keep from crashing into the Mustang.

They missed the Mustang, colliding into each other, setting off a chain of fender-benders up and down the avenue fronting the train station.

Charlie cried, "Oh, my God!"

Hank grinned. "Don't you just love it?!"

A woman pushing a baby carriage had to step lively to get out of the way of the oncoming Mustang, whose front fender missed grazing her backside by a hair.

Hank beeped the horn at her, chortling.

Charlie, appalled, said, "You're a sick fuck."

Hank tilted the rearview mirror so he could see himself in it, then stuck out his tongue. "Nyah, nyah, takes one to know one!"

Charlie shook his head in disgust. "You sick bastard."

Hank slammed on the brakes, throwing himself forward. The car skidded to a stop, halting a few feet away from the rear bumper of a car at a red traffic light at the intersection.

The driver of the other car swiveled in his seat, turning around, sticking his head out of the window and looking back to see what kind of idiot had narrowly missed crashing into him.

Hank opened the car door and grabbed himself by the collar. "I warned you."

Charlie said, "What are you doing?! Hank! Stop!—"

Hank tossed Charlie, that is, himself, out the car

and into the street. Charlie hit the asphalt, tumbling head over heels.

Seeing this, the driver in the car ahead of the Mustang decided that minding his own business was the better part of valor. He'd have driven away fast to get away from this nut, but another car stood in the lane ahead of his, blocking his escape. He told himself that he'd just sit tight and ignore the nutcase until the light changed.

Hank came out of a somersault, jumping to his feet, throwing himself back in the Mustang. Heedless of such minor impediments as traffic lights, he wheeled the Mustang across the dividing line, driving the wrong way down the oncoming traffic lane, angling across the intersection and away.

Irene's escape plan was no less problematic. The train's next stop was the South County station, where Charlie had arranged to have them met by some of his brother state troopers. But Boshane was on board the train, a killer, hunting her. Dickie was on board, too, hopefully still unconscious and stripped to his skivvies in the bathroom of the private compartment.

Irene certainly wasn't going to return to that compartment to take a look. She'd be safer up front, maybe, where there were other passengers in the dining car or coach cars. Or would she?

She moved forward, scurrying down the railroad car's central aisle, nervously glancing back over her shoulder. The corridor seemed like a too-long tube, a potential shooting gallery, with the closed compartment doors lining it on either side. Irene was alone in the aisle, rushing toward the rectangular door at the opposite end of the corridor.

On her left, a compartment door stood slightly ajar. Looking back, Irene thought she glimpsed a shadowy figure beyond the opposite end of the aisle, the way she'd come.

Taking the plunge, she stepped inside the compartment—it was empty.

With any luck, she could ride it all the way to South County station.

Looking around, she saw that one of the compartment's long walls was equipped with an overhead luggage compartment, not unlike those found on passenger planes.

Across the corridor, the door of the opposite compartment opened, its occupants stepping out into the aisle. They were four college kids, heading home for a visit. They went up the aisle, through the doorway at the car's forward end, heading for the bar car to get some brews and snacks.

No sooner had the door shut behind the last of them, then Boshane entered the car at the opposite end. All he saw was the door closing, and he hurried down the empty corridor toward it.

Nearing the forward end, he saw that a compartment door on his right was ajar, open about six inches. It was the compartment the college kids had just quit, but Boshane didn't know that. To his suspicious cop eyes, it looked promising. If it didn't pan out, he'd just keep on searching. And if he did find Irene, well, then—

He stuck his head inside the compartment. It was empty, but showed all the signs of recent occupancy, including scattered newspapers, magazines, traveling bags, CDs, an acoustic guitar, jackets and hats, and lots of other stuff.

That it had been occupied meant nothing to Boshane. The occupants were gone and Irene might have ducked in. Stepping inside, easing the door closed, he drew his gun.

First, he opened the bathroom door, but the space was empty. Back in the compartment, his eyes immediately went to the large overhead luggage compartment. Slowly, Boshane moved to it, his gun ready. His free hand reached for the overhead compartment handle. Suddenly, he yanked it open.

The compartment was filled with luggage, the bags stuffed in there as only a bunch of college kids could do. Their gear was crammed in there, overflowing to bursting, and only some miracle of muscle had compressed the bags enough to click the locker handle closed.

Now that it was opened, the bags, under pressure, came tumbling out, crashing down on Boshane. An oversized green duffel bag, stuffed with dirty laundry until the seams were bursting, flopped down on top of him, knocking him to the floor.

It was followed with a small, square, heavy camera case with metal reinforcements at the corners, one of which clonked Boshane square on top of his skull as he sat on the floor with the duffel bag weighing him down.

Boshane was knocked unconscious, so he didn't feel the tennis rackets and lacrosse raquets and pairs of Rollerblade in-line skates that rained down on him. But they all added their toll, and when he finally came around, he'd be hurting.

Hank's plan was simple, straightforward. He'd drive to the South County train station, meeting Irene there when she got off the train. The Mustang muscled along the highway, eating up the miles between it and Jamestown.

No problemo!

No?

Hank shuddered under the impact of Charlie's return. Sharing bodies was like trying to squeeze ten pounds of stuff into a five-pound bag.

Spirits sinking with a sickening feeling, Hank tilted the rearview mirror so he could see himself in it. Worse, he saw Charlie.

Hank said, "What the fuck are you still doing here?"

"You can't just throw me away, Hank. We're in this together," Charlie said, smug.

"Whatever, cupcake. Just keep your hands off my lady's pie."

That wiped the smugness off of Charlie's mug. He went ballistic. "Your lady?! You should be ashamed of yourself, buying rum and a dildo."

Unabashed, Hank fired back. "Oooh, that really cuts deep, coming from the watermelon-fucker."

Charlie, at least, had the grace to blush.

In Jamestown, at the South County train station, the police presence was limited to one state trooper, namely Trooper Finneran, who stood leaning against his car in the parking lot, arms folded across his chest, watching for the imminent arrival of the train he believed would be bearing Charlie and Irene.

Sunlight gleamed on the tracks, stretching into the distance, converging. Where they came together, a blur of motion appeared, steadily oncoming, the train sounding its whistle as it rolled into the station.

The deep-voiced conductor did his thing over the PA system on the train, announcing, "This stop, South County. South County, Rhode Island."

In a railroad car, in a seemingly empty compartment, the overhead luggage compartment's hatch clicked, opening up and out from inside. Curled within the space, legs and arms folded, body molded to the container, lay Irene.

She crawled out, lowering herself to the floor. Her body was stiff from being in that cramped position and she stretched, trying to work out some of the kinks.

Easing the compartment door open a crack, she

saw a small knot of people clustered around the open doorway of the opposite compartment. A blue-uniformed conductor stood there, and a brakeman, along with a couple of college kids in sweatshirts and jeans. The attention of all the assembled was directed inward, to something inside the compartment.

Nobody even noticed her as she stepped out, into the hall. Curiosity and perhaps a touch of intuition prompted her to peer over their shoulders, to see what was in the compartment.

Sprawled on the floor, half-buried under luggage, lay Agent Boshane, unconscious, a bloody gash in the corner of his forehead.

The railroad brakeman had already relieved Boshane of his gun, which he now held awkwardly, fumbling with it in his hands.

One of the collegiates, a shaved-skull dude with seventeen steel rings piercing the edge of one ear, who also sported a billy-goat goatee, was saying to the trainmen, "Yeah, we came back and found the dude like that. He must've been trying to rip us off. Serves him right, the prick."

The conductor said, "We'll turn him over to the police."

Irene turned, walking away, making for the far end of the corridor.

Meanwhile, in another car, Dickie Thurman had finally managed to extricate himself from being tied up earlier while he was unconscious. He wore a sleeveless undershirt, boxer shorts, and knee-length black socks.

He looked around the compartment for the rest of his clothes, but they were gone, along with his gun, all tossed out through the hole in the window.

Noises outside his door put Dickie on his guard. Stealthily he padded in stockinged feet to the door, easing it open a hairline crack, and peeking outside.

He caught a quick glimpse of a conductor coming down the aisle, alone.

Dickie ducked back, not wanting to betray his presence to the approaching trainman. As the conductor drew abreast of the compartment, the door opened and a hand shot out, grabbing him by the collar and hauling him off his feet, into the compartment.

The door slammed shut, while Dickie clubbed the hapless trainman into insensibility. Only when the conductor was stretched out unconscious on the floor, did Dickie realize that his quick glimpse of the man might have been a little too quick, since he now could see that the conductor was short, measuring less than five feet tall, and slightly built.

That presented a problem for Dickie, a big guy and no lightweight, but at least it made it easier for him to manhandle the unconscious body, rolling the pint-sized conductor around on the floor as he stripped him of his uniform.

Dickie pulled on the conductor's blue pants, feeling like he was stuffing himself into a sausage skin.

Forget about closing the top of the pants, he couldn't get the button close enough to the buttonhole to try it. Little worry about the pants falling down, though, not when they clung to him as tightly as a rubber girdle.

The cuffs ended about midshin, making the pants look like something a beachcomber would wear.

The conductor's tunic split at the shoulder seams when he pulled it on, his hairy forearms jutting well past where the short sleeves ended.

The shoes were small, causing Dickie intense discomfort as he crammed his feet into them. They fit his feet like half-slippers, with his ankles outside the shoes, crushing down flat the leather heels and uppers. They made Dickie look as if he walked on cloven hooves.

Glancing out the window, he saw Irene crossing the station platform.

Before detraining, Irene tied a scarf across the top of her head, then donned a pair of sunglasses. A few passengers were ahead of her, filing off the train. She followed them out, stepping down to the pavement.

Keeping her head down, trying to look as unobtrusive as possible, she quickened her pace, moving away from the train and the station building.

Someone came up behind her, pressing something hard into the small of her back. Irene gasped, her steps faltering.

The someone was Dickie Thurman, and the something that he was pressing against her back was his fingertip, but under the circumstances, she couldn't tell that it wasn't a gun.

Dickie nudged her from behind, moving her along. "Just keep walking, sweetheart."

Over her shoulder, she said, "You are such an asshole."

Dickie cut a ridiculous figure, walking along at a kind of shuffling gait necessary to keep the too-small shoes from falling off. The too-small conductor's uniform didn't help, either.

Another hitch appeared in the plan. Spotting Irene, Trooper Finneran started toward her. Because of the scarf and sunglasses, he wasn't absolutely sure it was she, and the guy walking behind her sure as hell wasn't Charlie, so Finneran started forward to check them out himself.

As Finneran neared, Dickie put on a great big bright smile. The trooper was eyeing Irene, trying to make an identification. While he stared at her, Dickie moved in suddenly from the side, sucker-punching Finneran, knocking him down.

Following him to the pavement, Dickie pounded the trooper a few more times, knocking him into a daze. Dickie unbuttoned Finneran's holster, scooping out his weapon.

Irene started to run, but Dickie had the gun, and when he called after her to stop, she did. He was too close to miss her if he fired.

Dickie came up alongside her, holding the gun

straight down at his side. Grabbing her upper arm, he started herding her to the sidelines, toward the edge of the station parking lot.

In another part of the lot, the red Mustang whipped in from a side street, screeching to a halt at the train platform. Not bothering to open the door, Charlie hopped out of the car, rushing to the platform as the train pulled out of the station.

Charlie made a fist, swinging it frustratedly in the air. "Shoot! She must've gotten off already."

From a distance, Irene's voice shouted, "Hank, help!"

Charlie whirled, turning in time to see Dickie hustling Irene down a side path toward the river. Burned up, he said aloud, "What am I, chopped liver?"

Hank kicked in, doing a vicious mimicry of Charlie's words. "What am I, chopped liver?"

Getting back to his normally obnoxious delivery, he barked, "Move your ass!"

Charlie took off after Irene and Dickie. "Let her go!"

Seeing Charlie, Dickie started hustling Irene away faster, half steering, half dragging her.

Charlie's progress across the station lot was suddenly interrupted by the appearance of Trooper Finneran, who'd somehow managed to get to his feet and stood reeling and weaving. Through blurred double-vision he recognized Charlie and moved to intercept him. "Hold it, Charlie, you're coming with me—"

Charlie punched the hulking Finneran in the mouth. It wasn't much of a punch, but there was even less left of Finneran after the walloping that Dickie had given him.

Floored, Finneran flopped to the pavement. Charlie continued his pursuit of Dickie and Irene. Running, he looked incredulously at his fist. "Did I do that?"

Determinedly unimpressed, Hank said, "Yeah."

"Wow. It was a lucky shot."

Beyond the edges of the station, the ground sloped down to the river, which rushed along a ten-foot-high, square-sided stone aqueduct that had once been an old canal. The river was about twenty feet wide. Farther down the channel, a couple of hundred yards away, a traffic bridge spanned the river.

For Dickie, that was too far. Much nearer, a metal cable pipeline stretched from side to side above the water, supported from below by a scaffolding of steel struts and crossbeams, their bases submerged by the swift-running water where they were set into the riverbed.

Across the river lay a parallel street, a district of houses and yards, and cars that could be commandeered at gunpoint.

Dickie herded Irene to the land's edge, where a smooth, wide concrete shelf stood, the top of the aqueduct wall. The sound of running water was loud.

Dickie looked back, seeing Charlie at the top of the slope, starting down toward him. Having no other choice, he forced a very nervous Irene to start crossing the pipeline ahead of him.

The pipe was about three feet in diameter, with a flimsy airplane cable railing set at waist-height above it, supported by upright posts at wide-spread intervals. The pipe was circular, its upper half rounded, tricky footing that made Irene edge forward with teeny-tiny steps.

The steel cable rail was too thin to dare leaning against, serving primarily as a handhold for repair crews to maintain their balance should they be called to work on the pipeline.

Below, the river rushed along, swift black waters with turbulent whitewater scallops whipping across its surface.

Poking Irene hard in a kidney with the gun barrel, Dickie forced her to continue forward, leaving the land behind as they made their slow creeping way across the pipeline.

Charlie, breathless, finally arrived at the trestle. Irene and Dickie were nearing the midpoint of the span.

He started after them—not. His left leg was frozen, immobile, rooted to the ground. Charlie hauled at it, but the damned thing wouldn't budge.

And he knew why. "Hank, what are you doing? Give me the leg!"

Enter Hank, with a pitying smile, shaking his head. "No way, Charlie. You swim like a bag of rocks."

Charlie couldn't believe what he was hearing. He again tried to make his move, only to have his inert left leg continue the deadlock.

Impassioned, he cried, "Cut it out, Hank! Irene needs us."

Hank spoke from the lofty heights of smug superiority. "That's right, Charlie. And that's called codependency and we deserve better."

"But this is Irene. I thought you were in love with her, too?"

Hank's smile was wan. "Well, love's a strong word. I mean, I love lots of things—baseball, for instance . . . and other broads."

Charlie said, "You fucking phony."

Hank shrugged. "Hey, any plays I called were for the good of the team."

"What about the lies about my father?"

"Look, I had the beaver in the trap and I just had to skin it. You're a guy, you know the drill."

"Then what about Whitey? The tears, the total insincerity. Come on."

"Hey, we needed a car—"

Charlie's right hand punched Hank's left leg. Hank said, "Auuggghhhh!"

This was the showdown. Charlie now knew that while a man who fights himself can never lose, he can never win, either.

Which meant that it was time to serve the eviction notice.

Charlie told his Hank-self off, but good. "You son

of a bitch! This is my body, do you understand that? I'm calling the shots from here on in. I don't need you to fight my battles. When you back down from something this important, you're nothing at all. *You're nothing at all!*"

Then, like a double image suddenly resolving itself into a singularity, the two selves of Charlie Baileygates merged into one, a unified wholeness.

Charlie looked out at the world through his own eyes, doing a solo act.

Hank was gone.

Just like that, Charlie's left leg unfroze, no longer binding him to the ground. He shook the leg loose, shaking it out. Sizing up the job ahead, he hesitated, but only for an instant.

Swallowing hard, he stepped up on to the pipeline, clutching the cable railing, starting forward across the trestle.

Movement reminded him that he'd punched his leg really hard, and it still hurt. "Ow."

He made his way forward, cutting the distance between himself and Dickie, whose slow progress was additionally hampered by having to herd Irene along ahead of him.

When Dickie looked back, he saw that Charlie was coming up fast.

Dickie turned, pointing the gun at Charlie. "Don't come any closer!"

Irene said, "Hank, help!"

Charlie gestured reassuringly, a casual but dan-

gerous move while walking a narrow trestle above
rushing black waters.

He said, "Don't worry, Irene. Hank's gone. It's
me, Charlie."

Irene's face fell. "Um, maybe you should go for
help."

"No. I can handle this."

Charlie moved closer still to Dickie. Dickie
pointed the gun directly at Charlie. He said, "I'm
warning you. You're gonna get hurt."

Moving a couple of feet closer, Charlie couldn't
have seemed more confident. "Somehow I don't
think so."

Dickie was sweating. It was the ultimate nightmare, confronting someone who was either too crazy
or too idiotic to be afraid of a gun. "Get back!"

But, even though Charlie had no gun, he had
something else, something inside him that was
stronger than lead slugs. That something was the
proud tradition and heritage of the finest law enforcement outfit in the U.S.—hell, the North Amer-
ican continent, with Hawaii, Guam, and the Virgin
Islands thrown in.

Charlie, smiling, held out his hand. "Come on,
Dickie. Give me the gun. No one ever gets away
from the Rhode Island State Police. Now it's over."

He reached for the weapon, to take it away from
Dickie. Dickie pulled the trigger, shooting Charlie in
the hand.

The gunblast was explosive, a thunderclap. Charlie swayed, looking down at his maimed hand. Something was wrong with it, but for an instant his stunned brain couldn't process the data.

Then it sank in. His four fingers were still intact, but he was now minus a thumb.

His smile was gone, too.

That did it. Charlie got mad. "*Goddammit*! All right, that's kidnapping and assault."

As Irene looked on in horror, Dickie raised the gun, pointing it at Charlie's face. He said, "Why stop there?"

Suddenly something struck him in the shoulder, hard, causing Dickie to stagger from the blow. Gasping, he let the gun slip from his nerveless fingers, dropping it into the water.

"Yeooww!" Dickie leaned forward in pain, glancing back at his shoulder. Buried deep in it, its four-inch-long steel needle tip firmly embedded in his flesh, was a bright red-and-green plastic, torpedo-shaped lawn dart.

Dickie croaked disbelievingly, "Jarts . . . ?"

He, Irene, and Charlie all turned to see who had thrown it. There, standing at the river's edge, was Whitey.

Reaching behind his back, clawing for the Jart, Dickie Thurman wobbled, losing his balance and tumbling headfirst off the trestle, into the river.

Instantly the raging black current whipped him away, downriver.

Being suddenly released from Dickie's viselike

grip caused Irene to lose her balance, too, and she fell into the river, vanishing from sight.

After a pause, her head bobbed into view, thirty feet downriver. Her arms thrashed, fighting a losing battle against the swift current, caught in a swirling eddy that spun her around instead of shooting her downstream.

Charlie hesitated, but only for a heartbeat. Then he jumped in after her.

Icy black water closed around his head, unseen underwater currents pulling at his limbs. Charlie flailed around, his dog-paddle style further hampered by the loss of his thumb and the shock and loss of blood attendant on such an injury.

His head broke the surface, and he splashed toward Irene, making for her. When he reached her, he was caught up in the whirling swirl, tossing the two of them together. Irene had swallowed a lot of water and was coughing it up, choking. In a panic, she grabbed the nearest buoyant object—Charlie's head.

Charlie did his best, but time and his energy were running out. It took all of his efforts to stay in one place and keep them from being whipped farther downstream. He didn't have enough left to break out and make for the sidewalls, whose smooth surfaces furnished no handholds to cling to.

Plus, he really couldn't swim, and he was having trouble breathing as Irene's frantic efforts kept pushing his head underwater.

Things were looking grim when suddenly the river's rushing sound was drowned out by something even mightier, a furious overhead whooping and whirling flood of noise that sounded like a giant egg-beater in the sky.

Hovering overhead was a New York State Police helicopter, but those aboard it were no mere minions of the law. In the cockpit were Charlie's three sons, Lee Harvey, Jamal, and Shonte Jr.

Secured by harness straps, Shonte Jr. leaned out of the cockpit's window, speaking through a bull-horn. Shonte Jr. said, "Hold on, Daddy. We's coming!"

Charlie, elated, was filled with new strength, allowing him to fight the current. "Irene, it's my boys!"

Working the control stick like a pro, Jamal positioned the copter directly over the two heads bobbing in the river. Lee Harvey threw a rope ladder over the side—after first making sure that his end of it was properly secured inside the aircraft.

The other end of the rope ladder drifted down to Charlie and Irene. Commandeering the bullhorn, Lee Harvey said, "Grab ahold of the motherfucker!"

Irene grabbed hold of the rope ladder, seizing the rungs with both hands. Charlie's hands weren't working so well, not with one of them missing a thumb, but he managed to hook his forearm over a rung, maneuvering himself into a secure hold.

Once they were safely fixed on the rope ladder,

the helicopter rose, hauling Charlie and Irene out of the river, lifting them to safety.

Standing at the river's edge, Whitey waved and cheered.

Chapter Thirteen

In the aftermath, police cars and ambulances thronged the riverside area, emergency lights flashing. Law enforcement agents swarmed the site, taking photos, making measurements, collecting evidence.

In the back of an ambulance, wrapped in blankets, seated side by side, were Charlie and Irene. The vehicle's rear hatch was opened, affording a view of the police activity along the riverfront.

Dr. Rabinowitz worked over Charlie's hand, cleansing then bandaging his bloody stump of a thumb. He said hopefully, "Are you going to able to save it, Doc?"

The healer snorted. "Save what? Your thumb's vaporized. You're lucky to be alive, you idiot."

"Well, that's something."

Captain Partington approached, accompanied by a sharp-eyed sleuth in a wheelchair. The captain said, "Irene, Charlie, this is Agent Steve Parfitt, FBI. He's an old friend from my U.S. marshal days."

Agent Parfitt said, "Nice to meet you." Facing Charlie, he said, "You must be awfully proud of your sons."

Jamal and Lee Harvey scuffed dirt with their shoes, embarrassed. Shonte Jr. said, "Hey, we proud of that motherfucker, too."

Charlie beamed. In an aside to Lee Harvey, Jamal whispered, "If he be getting any of that pussy, I be *real* proud of him."

Partington said, "When Lee Harvey called on the scanner and filled me in on his suspicions, I gave Steve a call."

Parfitt nodded. "We've been watching the EPA fellas for sixteen months. We knew they were dirty, but we hadn't connected them to the Dickie Thurman case."

Lee Harvey said, "What happened to those two crooked sumbitches we was butting heads with?"

"We scraped Gerke up off the pavement in Providence and Captain Partington nabbed Agent Boshane at the train station twenty minutes ago. Boshane's being kept on ice for a federal warrant which is on the way to him."

Charlie saw Whitey standing off to one side, being interrogated by a couple of state troopers. He hopped off the back of the ambulance, gathering the blanket folds around him as he crossed to the small group.

Facing the troopers, Charlie said, "Excuse me, could I have a word with my friend?"

They nodded, walking off. Charlie turned to the albino. "I owe you big-time, Whitey . . . but I do have mixed feelings, though."

Whitey said, "Why?"

"I'm just sorry you had to kill again. I know it must be hard after all you—"

"I never killed anyone before."

"Hm? But you said . . ."

"You were an admitted schizo who was wanted for murder and you're laying in bed next to me gabbing like we're old pals." Whitey shrugged. "I got scared."

Charlie, stunned, said, "But then, your family— how did they all die?"

"I never said they were dead, I said they were *gone*. They all moved to Phoenix. With my skin, I'd last about ten minutes out there."

Whitey stared at Charlie's chin, whose water-logged gauze and tape bandage was hanging by a thread. "Hey, your bandage is all wet."

Charlie picked at the last strands of tape. "Well, it's probably time to come off."

His three sons moved away from the ambulance, approaching Charlie from behind as he took off the bandage. Jamal said, "Hey, Daddy."

"Hm?" Charlie turned, facing them, revealing a grotesque Kirk Douglas-style dimpled chin that looked like somebody had poked a hole there with a pencil.

The Baileygates brothers froze, taken aback. Jamal said, "Holy shit! Look at Daddy. He got a goddamn butthole on his face."

Charlie and the lads all enjoyed a hearty laugh over that one. Charlie said brightly, "Oh, here we go."

Stepping up to the plate to take his turn at bat, Shonte Jr. said, "He sure is one Spartacus-looking motherfucker."

Charlie laughed again, mirthful.

Now Lee Harvey took his shot. "Hey, Daddy, now you can blow your nose and wipe your ass at the same time."

Charlie stopped laughing. "All right. That's about enough."

The brothers clammed up, abashed. Lee Harvey said, "Sorry, Daddy."

The next day, Charlie sat on the front fender of a car in the parking lot of the Castle Hill Hotel, Jamestown's finest. The sky was blue and so was he as he contemplatively studied the bandaged stump of his thumb, his rebuilt dimpled chin jutting out a mile.

The car was Irene's and she was busy at the other end, somberly loading some luggage into the car trunk. She said, "How'd your meeting with the shrink go?"

Charlie said, "Great. She gave me a clean bill of

health. I'm just another well-rounded individual."

Irene smiled. "That's great, Charlie. I'm really happy for you."

Closing the lid of the trunk, she moved around the car to the driver's-side door, pausing with her hand on the handle.

Charlie hopped off the car, coming around to her. "Well, Irene, if you're ever down these parts again, I, uh, I hope you'll look us up."

"Of course. I wouldn't think of going here without stopping in."

She smiled, a little sadly. The conversation stalled, developing into an awkward silence.

Irene said, "Little old Rhode Island."

Charlie nodded. "Biggest little state in the union."

"Well, goodbye."

"Yeah, goodbye."

Somehow he found the nerve to kiss her, a tentative little brush of the lips against her cheek.

Forcing a smile, she got into the car, looking up through the open window at him.

He said, "Hey, maybe I'll drop in on you sometime soon."

"Promise?"

Straightening up, standing tall, he gave her a snappy salute. "You bet. And that's the word of a Rhode Island State Trooper, ma'am."

Irene smiled.

The car started, slowly wheeling out of the parking lot, making a turn on to Main Street and driving down it, toward the entrance ramp to the highway.

There was some kind of obstruction ahead. Irene slowed the car. Standing ahead of her, in the middle of the road, was Captain Partington, motioning for her to stop, the other hand holding a bullhorn to his mouth.

Even if she'd gone around him, she couldn't have continued much farther, since the road was blocked by a half dozen or more Rhode Island State Police cars.

Through the bullhorn, Captain Partington blared, "Hold it right there!"

Handing the bullhorn off to Pritchard, the captain approached the driver's side of Irene's stopped car. Irene's face was taut, her hand clawlike as she ran stiff fingers nervously through her hair.

She said, "Oh, my God, this isn't happening. Tell me this isn't happening."

Partington's face was as warm and expressive as a concrete block. "Miss Waters, I'd like you to pop the trunk and step out of the car please."

"What?!"

"I think you heard me, ma'am."

Irene got out, her heels angrily click-clicking on the asphalt as she walked to the back of the car with Partington. She said, "Oh, this is hilarious. What did I not do now?"

The captain said, "We received a tip from the EPA that you might be transporting marijuana across state lines."

Impervious in her innocence, totally confident, Irene popped the trunk, lifting the lid. She said sarcastically, "Well, be my guest—"

Captain Partington nodded to Trooper Neely, who began rummaging around among the luggage, searching, peering, prying.

"—Have yourself a party," Irene concluded.

Trooper Neely pulled out a kilo-sized brick of pot, brandishing it triumphantly. "Found it, sir."

Irene was a study in total outrage, the wide gaping O of her astonished mouth seeming to take up half her face.

When she found her voice, she gasped, "What?! That's not mine."

Partington fixed his eyes on her, not blinking. "Sorry, ma'am, you're under arrest. I'm going to have to ask you to put your hands on the hood and spread your legs."

By now, Irene knew the drill. She turned, facing the car, bending over and assuming the position, her firmly rounded rump outlined under her skirt.

Partington began frisking her from behind, starting from the shoulders down, giving her a patdown.

Irene protested, "But I've never seen that before. Somebody planted that there."

"That's what they all say, ma'am."

Irene went into total annoyance mode. "Oh, you guys are beautiful. Why don't you just get it over with? Forget the trial. Just lock me up right now. Throw away the key and keep me here forever."

Charlie said, "That's just what I had planned."

Sometime during the frisking, Captain Partington had yielded pride of place to Charlie, who had continued the body search of the still-unsuspecting Irene.

Now, he spun her around, so they stood face to face. Pointing to the sky, he said, "Look."

Not so high overhead, a crop duster's propellor plane overflew the town, towing a sky banner that read WILL YOU MARRY ME, IRENE?

Seeing it, Irene beamed. "A-B-C-D-E-F-G-H-I-J-K-L-M-N-I-P-Q-R-S-T-U-V-W-X—why not?"

Smiling, she leaned forward, planting a big kiss on Charlie's lips. They embraced, going into a long, lip-locking kiss, after an initial instant's awkwardness in arranging their faces around Charlie's enormous new chin.

After that, the hugging and kissing proceeded without a snag.

Aloft, in the cockpit of the prop plane, were crowded Jamal, Lee Harvey, Shonte Jr., and Whitey, all outfitted with old-fashioned leather flying helmets. Shonte Jr. handled the piloting chores, Lee Harvey copiloted, and Whitey and Jamal sat in the rear seats. Jamal, who had a horror of anyone else's piloting but his own, leaned his face out over an open window, looking ill-at-ease.

Lee Harvey said, "That skinny-assed bitch better be reading this."

Whitey said, "I'm sure she sees it."

Ever the romantic, Shonte Jr. rhapsodized, "Yeah, it'll be raining wine and roses tonight."

Jamal, turning green, said, "It's gonna be raining my motherfucking cookies if you don't knock off this turbalence shit."

Down below, Trooper Finneran trudged off to his police cruiser, ready to start it up and go back on duty. It was all very well for Charlie and his broad to make out in the middle of Main Street under the approving eye of Captain Partington, but there were some serious and dedicated law enforcement professionals like himself who were devoted to a higher calling.

Lifting his gaze, tilting his square-jawed face skyward, as if seeking divine inspiration from the heavens, Trooper Finneran got dumped on big-time, spattered under huge steaming masses of stinking stomach bilge that slimed him from head to toe.

Jamal's upchuck had down-dropped.

Seeing Finneran staggering half blinded under the spew, a nearby trooper said near-admiringly, "Some birds!"

Indeed.

So ends the strange case of Charlie Baileygates, whose two selves came together when he fell in love with one very special woman.

He and Irene were married, and they all moved in together and lived as one big happy family—Charlie, Irene, the three brothers, and even Whitey.

It was a beautiful thing, a heart-warming affirmation of the triumph of the human spirit.

That is, until that night that Whitey, drunk and brooding, came home carrying a claw hammer. As it turned out, his family hadn't really moved to Phoenix after all—

But that's another story, for another time.